STEPHANIE ERICKSON

I0622707

THE HUMAN

CHILDREN OF WISDOM · BOOK 3

ISBN-13: 978-1-944793-03-6

Nothing escapes the will of God. Not even evil.

ONE

"It takes a special kind of person to control her own destiny. There are things beyond your reach, dear Mara. But you are a force to be reckoned with, and I know you will give the powers that be a run for their money."
— *Mara's grandmother's goodbye note to her*

Penn

Where is she?

Michaela had one assignment. One soul to collect. Reapers usually bring a few thousand souls home from Earth each day. But Michaela and I had been to hell and back, *literally*, so her boss decided to give her a much-deserved break.

Still, hours and hours have passed, and there's no sign of her.

Michaela isn't one to dillydally; she's compassionate, diligent, and ever a rule follower. Of course, the assignment she was given wasn't easy. The soul she was sent to collect was the latest of the surprises.

Reapers are rarely surprised. The Fates determine each human's lifespan, and when a person's allotted time runs out, their name appears on one of the Reaper's lists. The Reaper goes to Earth to collect the soul and brings them to their final rest-ing place. Nothing to it, right? Recently, though, surprise names started popping up on the Reapers' lists—souls that shouldn't have been collected for decades. This most recent surprise was a child, which meant Michaela had to take a little girl from her parent's arms. It wasn't something she was terribly keen on doing, but her only alternative was to let the girl wander the Earth as a ghost for all eternity. Rock, meet hard place.

But with only one soul to collect—and a child's soul, no less—she should've been back in no time flat. It shouldn't have taken her all day.

I try to convince myself it's okay—that she's just taking her time with the girl. Letting her have a few extra moments with her family. But that thought only reassures me for a few hours.

So, I consider a different possibility in a vain attempt to soothe myself. Maybe she's just in a meeting with Ryker or the other Reapers. Maybe she went straight from the gates of heaven to Ryker's office. At any rate, if she's in a debriefing, she should be done any second.

I've been pacing Michaela's quarters for hours now, waiting for her to come back. There's little here to distract me, and the only thing that halts my nervous movement is when the projection on the far wall changes to an image of New York City at night, in all its glittering beauty. Michaela has her projections set to display her favorite places on Earth. This image of New York is a new addition. Truth be told, it makes me miss my life on Earth. I enjoyed my time there, and as a banished soul and former Fate, I feel a bit out of place here in the heavens. Michaela is the one who brought me back to help solve the mystery of the surprises. And without her, I'm not sure I can.

I resume my pacing when the image fades to a waterfall surrounded by lush greenery. My thoughts spiral downward into one worst-case scenario after another.

Horatia and Galenia, my sister Fates, slip into the room so quietly I almost don't notice them.

"She's not here." Galenia makes the observation in her soft voice as she scans the room with clear blue eyes.

"Yes, she is. We're just playing a rousing game of hide and

seek. Care to join us?" I say, continuing my pacing.

"Now, now," Horatia says as she goes to her sister's side. "We're all a little worried."

My head jerks up, and I give my sisters a closer look. Horatia is striking with her dark hair spilling around her shoulders and down her back. Her arms are wrapped around Galenia, who's smaller and more fragile looking, but no less lovely. Both of their faces are etched with concern.

"We felt certain she would be back by now. I didn't even consider an alternative," Horatia offers.

"Me neither. But I've been stewing in here for so long, I've come up with some doozies," I say as I turn away from them.

"Maybe it's not time to panic yet. She might just be taking her time with this one. She was sent to collect a child, and that requires a certain amount of delicacy," Galenia offers.

"All day?" I ask.

They don't answer right away.

"Maybe she's debriefing with Ryker," Horatia offers.

"I've thought of that," I say with a nod. "But if she is, she should come through that door any minute."

The three of us are silent for a few moments while we stare at the door. None of us wants to admit she isn't coming through it any time soon.

Eventually, I sigh and turn away. "Where's Webber? Still sitting at the cauldron, trying to make up for lost time?" Webber replaced me after I was banished to Earth. Once I was the greatest Fate the heavens had ever seen. My sisters and I were quite a team—while I spun the threads of life, Horatia cut them, and Galenia decided how they ended. Webber had angled for my job for years, but fate, as it happens, wasn't kind to him. He's not the Spinner he once claimed he'd be.

Horatia shrugs. "He said he wanted some time alone to recoup."

"I don't blame him for that," I say, trying not to think about my banishment, my human friends' untimely deaths, my unsanctioned return to the heavens, and our two trips to hell. We had to leave Webber there the first time, but we managed to rescue him and most of the souls in the prison of souls. Of course, the two who were left behind are very important to me. Kismet and Andrew, my friends. My best creations.

"I'm a little worried about Webber to be honest," Galenia says.

"Of course you are, you're basically the only one who cares about him at all," I say, not meaning to hurt anyone, just stating what I consider to be a simple fact. Webber is hard to like, even for someone like Galenia, who can find something to like about everyone. He's rude, pompous, and he tries too hard. Frankly, I could do without him in my life.

Horatia nods, but I'm not sure which one of us she's agreeing with. "Things didn't go well today at all, Penn. I'm not sure if it's because of his time in hell, or because he knows he's on his way out. Maybe both? But it was a bad day."

"How bad?"

"Our worst yet. Less than a hundred new souls were made."

I stagger back onto the stark white couch lining the side wall. "That won't keep up with the death rate, especially when you factor in the surprises. It will be a compounding problem." At our peak, the girls and I could create around two million souls per day. Granted, a day here in heaven is much longer than its equivalent on Earth, but that makes Webber's number even more staggeringly low.

They don't answer me. They already know this, and they're the ones who will have to deal with the situation now that I've lost my rank.

"How long until his replacement is ready?" I ask.

"We don't know. We don't even know if they've picked someone out for the job. Everyone is a little distracted right now," Horatia answers.

"Fair enough. But this can't go ignored forever. The population will suffer. The humans will notice the problem."

"I don't think it will go on for much longer," Galenia says quietly as she stands in front of the projection, looking as if she wants to touch the vibrant hummingbird painted on the wall before her.

"What do you mean?" I ask, not sure I want the answer.

"This level of stress and failure can't be maintained. The situation will come to a head. Soon," she says, keeping her eyes on the bright green bird as she tucks a strand of her long, brown hair behind an ear.

I want to say something light, funny, and hopeful. But I'm all out of quips. I'm also at a loss. Is she talking about the end of *everything*? Can that be possible? The end of the Earth has long been predicted, but when that happens, a new creation is meant to take its place. And production on that has not even started. Did I prematurely trigger the end of the world with my mistake? The question weighs heavily on me as I sink back into Michaela's couch.

We sit in silence together, my sisters flanking me on either side, as the minutes tick past.

Michaela still doesn't return.

TWO

Michaela

It's darker than anything I've ever experienced before, and I've been to hell and back. Recently. I blink my eyes, making sure they're not closed.

The air is cold and damp in the darkness, and a shiver rolls through me, making me very aware of the fact that my arms are tied behind my back around some kind of square post. The corners dig into the insides of my arms. My legs are splayed straight out in front of me, and the ground I'm sitting on is cold and hard. I move my leg a little bit, searching for something, anything. The surface beneath me is smooth, not like a tile floor would be. As my dress bunches and the bottom part of my calf is exposed, I can feel grit rolling beneath it. It's almost like I'm sitting on bare cement.

I turn my head left and right, searching for a source of light, but I find nothing. I'm blinking rapidly, if only to assure myself that my eyes are indeed open.

What happened?

Scanning my mind, I search for the last thing I remember. The girl. Lily. The gates of heaven. The Archangels. "Oh, God," I whisper, but He doesn't answer me.

They just disappeared in front of me. She simply reached out and grabbed their shoulders. I can still see the confused looks on their faces as they disintegrated. I've never seen anything like that happen to such powerful beings. Frankly, I hope to never see it again.

I remember Nathair, and the girl crying out for me to save her. And Mara... Who could forget her? The angry human responsible for savaging the tapestry of life. She severed several of the carefully spun threads of life, ending the humans' lives decades too soon, and then trapped their souls in that horrible prison in hell.

Tears form in my eyes. I've failed. Again. Despite all the precautions I took, the child's soul did not go to heaven where she belongs. Children are not unheard of in hell. Some are just black threads. But they are rare to say the least. And it is an absolute crime against humanity for a child who was meant for heaven to be condemned to even a moment in hell. Guilt washes over me—I promised to save her, but I didn't.

To my surprise, Nathair breaks my despair. He opens a small, rectangular slit—a window?—in what appears to be a door. The sound of scraping metal makes me want to press my hands to my ears, but I'm quickly reminded of my bound hands.

The light streaming in through the hole is absurdly bright, but I struggle to keep my eyes open, wanting to get a feel for my surroundings while I can. But the light is blinding, so I turn my face away from it, looking instead at the walls around me. It's a square room with no windows besides the one in the door. It's the world's smallest basement. There's nothing in here but the post and me. No shelving for storage, no canned goods, boxes of mementos, nothing. Just the post, me, and now Nathair on the other side of the door.

"Nathair! What's going on? Why are you helping her? We were made to protect the humans—to bring them *home*—not to destroy them," I plead with him. He scans the room silently before his dark eyes fall on me.

I see the tops of his shoulders bob above the bottom of the window in a shrug. "I just came to check on you, not debate good and evil."

"Nathair. Please," I beg, but his blank eyes tell me nothing. He slams the window shut, plunging me back into darkness. Once again, I'm rendered blind. But at least I have my bearings now. I know there's a door in front and bare walls to either side of me. If I can ever get free of my restraints, I will know where to start walking.

I've never cared much for darkness. Although Webber once made a strong argument that without it, it would be impossible to appreciate and recognize the light, now that I'm submerged in it, I can't help but relate to Penn's desire to minimize it within the world.

Something tells me that I'm not in hell. For one thing, the basement lacks that distinctive sulfuric odor. In fact, it's almost…earthy.

"They have me on Earth," I say to the darkness. The room is so damp that it swallows my words without leaving an echo behind.

Why trap me on Earth? They must know I can come and go as I please from here. If Mara doesn't understand that, certainly Nathair—as a fellow…well, former Reaper—would have explained our duties and privileges to her.

The quickest way out would be to call the mists and disappear into them. But no matter how much I relax, no matter how much I need them, they don't come. Normally, all I have to do to get them to appear is visualize them. The fact that it's not working makes my heart race. It also makes me feel incredibly vulnerable, which isn't an emotion I'm used to feeling. I can certainly empathize with the human souls I collect, but I'm a heavenly being. I'm not susceptible to any real threats. Until the Fates and I went to hell to retrieve those souls, I had never known real danger. But at least I had them. This horrible isolation is so much worse.

"I'm alone," I whisper, and my words are once again swallowed by the damp darkness.

Time stretches before me like some horrible unknown. With no sun or moon, no workday, nothing to give me any indication of how long I've been down here. Despair is my constant companion.

I think about Mara's last words to me—she'd told me I would help her, like it or not. But how? Surely keeping me tied up in this dank basement can't be the entirety of her plan. There's more to this situation than meets the eye, and it makes me wary.

Left to my own devices, I replay the memory of losing Lily again and again. Of course, I don't know what really happened to her—I don't remember anything after Nathair grabbed me—but I don't trust that this woman, Mara, would do right by her. After all, why else would she have been lying in wait?

How is she even doing this? Is she the one blocking the mists, or is Nathair helping her? She's human; her aged face attests to that. But that doesn't mean she's not powerful. When I think about the way those Archangels vanished… Well, it's obvious our foe is much more formidable than we originally anticipated.

The thing is, humans aren't supposed to know about our world.

But she does, and she vanquished two huge Archangels with no more than a touch.

I shiver again against the thought. *Diligence*, I remind myself. Just yesterday—in heavenly terms, at least, I met with God in his own personal Garden of Eden. He'd told me that my work was only just beginning. Diligence was the only way I'd see it through to the end.

The thought gives me strength. After all, diligence doesn't leave room for despair. I wiggle my wrists. They're tied together so tightly they're starting to ache. The coarse rope is making my skin itch, and my squirming only makes it worse. My shoulders are sore from the awkward position. I'm ready to be free—I *need* to be free—but my wiggling doesn't gain me an inch. Still, I have nothing but time stretched out ahead of me for what seems like an eternity. So I keep working. Keep squirming.

It's not quick, and it's not easy. It feels like a week passes as I struggle with my bonds, but it's probably only a few hours. The more I struggle, the weaker the rope gets. I just have to keep working at it. *Diligence.*

Eventually, I manage to wiggle my right hand just enough to give myself some leverage. I'm not out completely, but I know I'll be home free soon. But my shoulders are screaming, and each movement makes it worse. Still, I know I can't stay here. I can't give up. My work isn't done. I have souls to save and a human to stop.

One arm comes free first, and I slowly bring it around to the front of my body. I can almost hear the creaking in my shoulder. The urge to groan is almost impossible to resist, but I have no concept of the rest of the building, and I don't want to draw attention to myself. The last thing I need is for Nathair to come check on me. I'd be right back where I started if that happened. Or worse.

I have no idea what they'd do to me. The worst-case scenario ends with me joining the Archangels she made disappear, wherever they went. I shudder at the thought, determined not to let that happen.

I sit for a moment and revel in my almost freedom, but my left hand is still tied to the pole. Sighing, I extend my free arm back behind me to help untie my other hand, pushing past the pain in my shoulder.

It only takes a few moments, but it's a few too long for my aching body. Once both hands are free, I rub my wrists and bend over, bringing my knees up so I have a place to rest my head.

Now what?

My unseeing eyes search the darkness. The way out is just a few paces in front of me. But this isn't hell, where all the doors are open. Most who are brought there truly have no hope of escape—the apparent freedom is yet another form of torture—so I probably can't just open it and walk out of here. On second thought, I suppose this is what it feels like for the prisoners in hell. The doors may be open, sure, but what's on the other side might be more frightening than what is inside. After seeing what Mara did to the Archangels, I'm very aware that I'm not invincible. Frankly, I'd like to avoid her if I can.

But then I scold myself. I can't avoid her forever. I need to get her to stop this madness. But I can't face her alone either.

Making up my mind, I nod. I need to escape and get reinforcements. Just like I did after I discovered the prison of souls in hell.

It's comforting to have a plan of action, and it gives me the boost I need to rise to my feet. I dust off my long, black-and-white dress on impulse. I can't actually see it, but I just feel dirty after sitting on the gritty floor for so long.

Taking slow, measured steps, I approach the door with my arms outstretched in front of me.

After a few short steps, I make contact with what I think is the door. It's cold and smooth. I feel around, running my hands all over it, finding its outline among the cinderblocks.

There's not even a handle on this side. But I push the rising despair back down. Keep moving. Keep working. Stay focused. Diligence. It's my mantra as I feel for the slot in the door, hoping I can pry it open.

Hope is all I have in the darkness, and it's lighting my way as my fingers find purchase in the door.

THREE

Penn

The night drips on with a slowness that is painful, like trying to fill a gallon jug with a leaky faucet. It fills the three of us with dread because Michaela still hasn't returned. By now, we know she isn't in a meeting with Ryker. She isn't taking her time with her quarry. She didn't stop to admire a particular waterfall on Earth. She's in trouble.

"We have to do something," I say, standing so abruptly from my seat between my sisters that Galenia lets out a small gasp.

"What do you propose?" Horatia asks.

"I think we should go to the Reaper's wing and start asking questions. Someone must have heard something."

Galenia eyes me. "I don't think that's such a good idea. What if you're recognized?"

"I can't sit still any longer," I say. "We all know something went wrong."

"Why don't Horatia and I go?"

But the thought of waiting alone in Michaela's room makes me panic a little. Okay, more than a little. It fills me with a sense of dread so cold I physically shiver. "No. I'm coming too."

"How are two Fates and a Keeper going to avoid suspicion?" Galenia asks, clearly skeptical of my demand.

"It's late. There probably aren't too many people wandering around anyway," Horatia points out.

"Galenia raises a good point," I say. "It would be more inconspicuous if only one of us went. And since you two are joined at the hip, I should be the one to go."

"Since when do you care about being inconspicuous?" Horatia asks.

Before I can put together a solid argument, Galenia says, "No. We go together or we wait and see. No in between. We've been to hell and back together, we can certainly manage the Reapers' wing." There's a fire in Galenia's eyes I wasn't expecting. It assures me I've lost this battle. They're coming with me.

As we make our way toward the naming room, the place where the Reapers gather before setting out each morning, I struggle to maintain my composure. The gravity of what her disappearance might mean makes my feet feel like lead and my breath huff out in short gasps. I can't lose her. I can't add her to the list of losses I've incurred since this all began. My job. My home. Andrew. Kismet. No, I can't lose Michaela too.

It's eerily quiet in the corridors. Soon, we find out why. All the Reapers are packed into the naming room.

"Is it normal for them to be gathered at this time of night?" Horatia asks, but from her concerned tone, I can tell she already knows the answer. We all do.

Through the glass doors, I can see them gathered in front of the podium as Ryker addresses them from on high. But I can't hear what he's saying. I search the crowd for Michaela. None of the Reapers are facing us, but it doesn't matter. None of them share her long, blonde hair, her medium stature, or her glowing smile.

Relief wraps around me like a warm blanket when my eyes land on a Reaper with hair similar to Michaela's. I will her to turn around. It has to be her. Who else could it be? I'm smiling, planning what I'm going to say to guilt-trip her for worrying us, when the woman turns. Her face is sharp, coming to a point at her chin, with deep brown eyes and skin darker than Michaela's.

Disappointment doesn't even begin to describe the feeling that washes over me.

Ryker is still talking. His facial expressions reveal nothing. He's a stern man with a hard exterior, which means we're not going to learn anything from watching him speak. We need to hear what he's saying. But if one of them recognizes me, I'm done for. As a banished soul, if I'm discovered back in heaven, the punishment will be annihilation. Besides, if they spot the two Fates, they're bound to ask questions. It's lose-lose as far as I can see.

I sigh. I'm tired of living in a state of constant fear. It's exhausting. But even though I want to live, I'm not willing to live like *this*. Anyway, Michaela stuck out her neck to bring me back here. The least I can do is stick my own out for her.

Throwing caution to the wind, I slip into the naming room, with the Fates right on my heels. With any luck, the Reapers won't notice. But I've been in here before in my Keeper's uniform. Perhaps, if pressured, I can concoct a similar story about collecting information for the Keepers' records. Maybe even ask about the whereabouts of the latest missing Reaper. Nathair still hasn't been found, and the thought makes me shiver as I wonder if he and Michaela met with a similar fate.

That doesn't explain the two Fates' presence, but I'll deal with that if I have to.

We linger near the door in case we need to make a fast getaway, but Ryker's booming voice carries to the far corners of this room. He certainly is an intimidating presence, but I know Michaela has a soft spot for him, so there must be more to him. Then again, she has a soft spot for everyone, Webber included.

"Two Archangels have gone missing as well." His statement rings through to the back of the room, striking me right through the heart.

Archangels? They are supposed to be the strongest of all of us. If someone managed to best *them*, the entire world as we know it is in danger. Galenia's right. This situation *is* coming to a head. Now.

I swallow hard, trying to hold back a rising sense of panic.

Panic isn't my thing, and besides, it won't help at all.

Ryker's voice brings me back to the naming room. "Their disappearance is believed to be connected with Michaela's. We're doing everything we can to locate her, and we'll keep you updated as more information becomes available."

The Reapers erupt with questions—their voices a dull roar in the back of my mind. Or maybe that is just the blood rushing to my head. *Michaela's disappearance.*

As if of its own accord, my hand reaches past Galenia and finds purchase against the glass, bracing myself against the news.

She's really gone.

FOUR

Michaela

I hold still for a few moments, listening hard for any kind of sound on the other side of the door. My fingers grip the slat in the metal as if it's my only lifeline. I hear nothing at all, only the heavy sound of my own breathing. But I have no idea if that's because the door is soundproof, or if it means there's no one on the other side. Would they leave me unguarded? There's only one way to find out.

Worming the pads of my fingers into the small space between the slat and the door, I ease the small window open, millimeter by millimeter, until I have a firm hold. I pause, listening again, but there's still nothing. I try to ease it open as quietly as possible, but it makes that same screeching metal-on-metal sound, and the slower I move, the longer it drags out. Acting on impulse, I push it open hard. The sound echoes as if bouncing off walls that are too close together. I can only hope no one else heard it.

Blinking, I peer out the window, but the darkness outside is as absolute as it is in the room. When Nathair checked on me, there was light streaming in. Why is it so dark now?

I can only hope this isn't simply a smaller interior room in a larger basement that's guarded by another locked door. Before I can slump over with despair, I shake my head. No. I can't harp on everything that might go wrong. This is my opportunity to act.

Moving carefully, with tentative movements, I stick my arm out of the opening, hoping that if I can't see anything outside the door, then a potential guard can't see me either.

Pushing myself all the way to the edge of the window, I stretch my arm out as far as it will go, reaching for the edge of the door. Trying to find some sort of handle. When I don't find anything, I move to the other side. My hand finds purchase, and I almost buckle with relief. There's a knob on some kind of slider, and above it, a deadbolt. That's as far as my arm will reach, so if there's another lock under the knob, I won't know until I try to push the door open.

First, I try to undo the deadbolt, but it protests. It feels unused, not to mention displeased with the movement. It cries out with another scraping metal sound as it slams home. Trying to keep panic at bay, I feel for the other lock with a shaking hand.

Holding my breath, I brace my body against the inside of the door and pull the slider toward me. At first, it doesn't budge, and I fear it's rusted shut. How long have I been down here? Is it over? Has the world been destroyed and condemned to eternal darkness? I channel my panic into the lock, pulling as hard as I can.

Just as my darkest thoughts start vying to take over my mind, I feel the slider budge. A little. Then a little more. Until it too screams in protest as it slides free of its hold.

The door isn't rusted like the locks were, and it comes open more easily than I would have expected. Before I know it, I find myself in a heap on the floor. Outside the room. My hands go to the sides of the doorframe, and I pull myself up on shaky legs.

The glee I felt after escaping the hand restraints was nothing compared with this feeling.

But the darkness—so absolute it makes me feel blind—is eerie.

Pausing to assess my situation, I use my other senses. The

wall beyond the door is cement cinder blocks, just like the walls in my cell. I trace the grooves between the blocks in a straight line ahead of me as I shuffle forward. The air out here isn't much different than it was inside my room—another indication that I haven't escaped much of anything quite yet.

Each small step I take forward brings me closer to the certainty that Nathair will find me. That Mara will appear out of nowhere. That I will be trapped once more. But I'm not caught yet, and that thought is enough to keep me moving.

My foot abruptly connects with something, and I stumble forward before landing hard on a staircase. It feels bare beneath my hands, the wood splintered in places. Lucky for me, it leads upward, not deeper into the darkness. On hands and knees, I climb slowly, making a tremendous amount of noise. Each step creaks under my weight, and I get tangled in my dress more than once. It's harder than you might think to crawl up the stairs in a long dress in total darkness. Dignity and grace are definitely not my companions, but at least I'm moving forward. Toward what, I don't know, but it has to be better than going back into that dark prison, right?

Thankfully, the staircase is closed in on both sides by cinderblock walls, so it's not possible to topple off the edge. Using my hands to guide me, I make my way up the stairs until I can go no further. Another door.

I slowly pull myself up and brush off my no doubt filthy dress. Taking a deep breath, I steel myself for what's to come. I've tried not to think of it, but there's a very real possibility that this door may be locked.

My hand hits the door hard, making a thump as I reach out for a doorknob. I've never felt such a compulsion to swear. But swearing is for humans and Fates who've spent too much time on Earth. I smile, thinking of my dear friend, Penn, take a deep breath, and slowly feel for the doorknob. My fingers crawl across the surface until I find a lever—long, slender, and cold. Wrapping my hand tightly around it, I hold on for dear life.

I bring my other hand up to the doorframe and brace myself as I push the lever down slowly, waiting to feel resistance that never comes. This door must be newer than the one downstairs; it doesn't make a sound as I push it all the way down. All that's left to do is push it open and seize my freedom. Or so I hope.

With agonizing care, I push the door open, and the light that streams through the tiniest little slit I've made in the doorway blinds me.

FIVE

Penn

There's movement. It takes a Herculean effort, but I raise my head in an attempt to process what's happening around me. The Reapers are dispersing. Horatia and Galenia are pulling at me, forcing me into movement. I let them, and we slip out the door before a wave of Reapers descends on us.

We walk back toward Michaela's quarters in silence. It follows us inside, hanging heavy in the air, making our movements slow and my thoughts slower.

I'm afraid to break the silence. She's gone. If I say it out loud, it's like I accept it. And I don't.

I'm not sure why, but my panic is more absolute now than when I lost Kismet. Part of it is that Michaela is a heavenly being, so she should be immortal, infallible. Death is an integral part of human life, but not of ours. I shouldn't have to worry about losing her; she's an absolute. And yet, she's gone.

At the same time, I know there's more to it. Michaela has grown more important to me than I realized.

Horatia is our go-getter. Surely, she will have a plan. But she's disturbingly quiet. It's Galenia who finally breaks the silence.

"What can we do?" The despair in her voice makes something inside of me snap.

"We know who's responsible for this...for everything that's gone wrong lately. I say we find her and put an end to her interference. Now."

They aren't following me. "Who?" they ask in unison, bewildered expressions on their faces.

"*Mara*," I shout, giving voice to the unspoken fear we're all harboring. Someone may overhear me, but I can't bring myself to care. I'm done hiding. "The human."

Galenia lets out a gasp. "How can you be sure?" she asks.

"Come on, Galenia. She's the one who captured the surprises in the prison of lost souls. Andrew identified her by name. Michaela goes to collect the latest surprise and disappears herself? It's not that much of a leap to conclude that Mara has her."

"No." It's barely a whisper, but there's a look of pure terror on Horatia's face.

I'm not sorry for speaking uncomfortable truths, but I am sorry for scaring her.

Clasping Horatia's hands in mine, I say, "This is not the time to despair. We need to take action." Her expression doesn't change, and I fear I've lost her, if only for this moment.

"All we've done is take action, Penn, and look where it's gotten us."

Galenia is at my side in an instant, and she adds her hands to mine. "Penn is right, Ratia." She reaches up and gently wipes her sister's tears away with her thumbs. "There is no place for despair here. Only devotion."

Horatia takes a deep breath, and my relief is immense as I watch her despair harden into resolve. In all the years we've known each other, I've never seen her crack like that before.

"So, what do we do?"

"I need to get into the weaving room," I say.

The two Archangels who stand in front of the weaving room door look intimidating, but we have no choice except to face them. When the damage to the tapestry was discovered, Archangels were stationed outside at all times. Although it hasn't stopped the threads from being cut, it has strengthened the resolve of the guards. Getting past them won't be easy. But, the night is waning, and Michaela might not have much time left.

We have no plan for dealing with the guards. We just boldly march up to them. I'm at a loss for what to say, but Galenia comes to the rescue.

"This Keeper has come to see the tapestry for his records. He needs to chronicle the damage."

"Why didn't he come during the day?" one of the Archangels asks. Ever the stereotypical angel, he's huge and blond. He and his equally enormous partner are standing wingtip to wingtip, blocking the whole door.

"The Keepers asked me to come now so I won't be underfoot while the Weaver works."

The angels look skeptical, so I press my case. "They suggested I bring the two senior Fates to supervise."

The angel on the right eyes me carefully. "You seem very familiar, Keeper. Have we met before?"

I shift my weight, resisting the urge to face him head on. If he keeps looking at me, there's a good chance he'll identify me. Given my status, it would be his right to eliminate me on the spot.

I start wishing we'd thought this through a little more.

"Please," Horatia says, "we're very behind, and we'd like to get started a little early this morning if possible. The quicker this Keeper gets in and out, the better off we'll all be."

To my relief, the angel shifts his attention to her.

Both of the guards sigh. "Fine," the suspicious one says, "but if another thread is cut while you're in there, we'll know who to blame."

The threat gives me goose bumps.

"Believe me. If we see him cutting threads, we'll let you take care of him," Horatia says, clapping a hand on the angel's shoulder as we walk by.

I stifle a snort at the gesture and clear my throat, hiding my face behind the hood of my Keeper's uniform.

Galenia shuts the door behind us, and I hope it will offer enough privacy. But she still speaks in a whisper as we cross the room together and come to a stop in front of the tapestry of life.

"What now?"

Rather than answer her, I head straight to the tapestry, edging so close my nose almost touches it. I remember spinning Mara's thread not so long ago. The order for her was simple: *Highly intelligent but morally wayward.* I'll never forget that. How do you spin such a soul? But I did my best, and, inevitably, her thread turned out grey.

I start at the edge of the tapestry and work my way back toward Kismet's sparkling pink thread. It would've been before Kismet, but not too much before her. Eventually, I find Nysa's frayed thread, and there's my clue—Mara's intersects with it not long before the cut.

"There you are, you little devil." The sight of the thread fills me with a sense of dread. I wove it gray. I know that like I know my own name, but it has turned as black as the night. I trace it up the tapestry until it fades to the gray I created. In all my years as a Spinner, I've never seen anything like it.

"What happened to her?" Galenia asks.

"I don't know. And I don't need to know. We just need to find her."

I start at the end.

SIX

Michaela

Blinking in the light, I look around, waiting impatiently for my eyes to adjust, relying on my other senses to inform me of danger. But it's strangely silent.

The door opened to a hallway painted yellow. It's so warm and welcoming it's hard to believe it's connected to my prison. I choose to go left, toward what I can only assume is the back of the building.

Pictures line the walls of the hallway. Mara is in some of them, but a small boy is in all of them. He is young, only about six years old in the most recent picture, but based on how Mara looks in the photos, they're all at least two years old. The human had lines around her eyes when I saw her at the gates of heaven, but in these photos, she does not. Both mother and son look happy, and Mara is even smiling in one or two of them. But she's also watching the boy like a hawk, as if she's waiting for something to doom him, as if she's ready to stop it. The confidence behind her fierce gaze is puzzling. Most humans know they can't hold back their future, whatever it may hold. But if I've learned one thing about our adversary, it's that she can't be described by the word normal.

Like the memories I share with the souls I lead through the mists to the heavens, these images are telling me a story. Of days at the beach, the park, Christmases, birthdays, Halloweens, time with friends, time alone, and everything in between. Despite the circumstances, they make me smile. At one time, this was a happy family, however small it was. As I think about the hateful woman who stood before me at the gates of heaven, I can't help but wonder what happened to Mara.

A beeping sound interrupts my train of thought and stops me in my tracks. It's both steady and unobtrusive. But the way it drones on reminds me of a hospital.

I follow the sound to a door in the hallway. It's nothing special. Probably a bedroom or something on the other side.

My hand hovers over the doorknob as I look left and right down the hallway. I'm still alone. But am I inviting discovery by going inside? Shouldn't I focus on leaving? But whether it's a mistake or not, something about the beeping draws me to the room. I lower my hand onto the handle, gently push it down, and go inside.

A little boy lies on a bed along the far wall. He's unmistakably an older version of the child in those photographs. His eyes are closed and a heart monitor beeps steadily at his side. The room clearly belongs to him. It's painted blue with the Millennium Falcon emblazoned on the far wall. The dresser in the corner is topped with a television and the latest gaming console. But it's dusty, as if it hasn't been touched in a while. A window lets dappled sunlight in next to a large bookshelf, overflowing with books on every subject. He has *The Boxcar Children*, *Origami Yoda*, *Percy Jackson*, and *Harry Potter*. I smile at his collection as I walk around the room.

Finally, I turn to face the bed. I jump, startled, bringing my hand to my chest. There's a plush armchair in the far corner of the room, directly next to the bed. And the boy is sitting in it, or at least a reflection of him. He isn't a ghost. He's not silvery enough for that. He's like an opaque copy of himself. Realization hits me like a freight train. It's his soul—not quite a ghost, but not at home either.

I've never seen a soul trapped this way. Either they're ghosts on Earth or they're in transit to their final homes. But this... it makes my breath catch in my throat. It's wrong on so many levels. How long has he been like this? And how much longer can he last this way? Indefinitely? Hours? I can't decide for sure which option is worse.

The boy in the chair gives me a sad smile from under brown hair that's gotten long enough to cover his eyes. He tosses it back with a shake of his head and waves at me. But when he brings his hand up, I notice something thin attached to it. Following it with my eyes, I trace it all the way back to his body. I walk around the bed, my eyes glued to the shimmering thread, and the closer I get, the clearer it becomes.

Kneeling down in front of the boy, I study the surprises' threads. They're the ones Mara stole from the tapestry. Spotting Kismet's sparkler isn't hard. It's right there, braided in with the rest. The rope—if you can call it that—is crude and frayed, but it's doing its job. It's keeping him here.

"I'm Shiloh," the boy's soul says to me. It startles me out of my trance, and I look up at him.

"Hi, Shiloh. It's nice to meet you. I'm Michaela."

Mara's cryptic words echo in my mind. *Everything* will *be okay, for my son Shiloh. You're going to help me save him.*

The pieces fall into place as I put it all together. Mara is stealing threads to save her son. He was probably meant to die a while ago, judging by the look of his soul.

The weight of it pushes me down onto the bed, and I sit facing this little boy's soul.

"I'm surprised to see you here. Reapers don't come here, except Nathair of course, but he didn't come to take me home."

His frankness startles me almost as much as the fact that he knows what I am. "Home? Isn't this your home?" I ask, trying to avoid the elephant in the room.

"Well, no. Mom is keeping me here. I got sick a couple of years ago, but she figured out how to keep me here." He shrugs quickly, and the second-nature gesture reminds me of his youth and innocence. "I don't blame her. We had so much fun before

I got sick. When Dad died, I think it was kinda hard on my mom. I was little, so I don't really remember it. But she worked hard to make sure I had a happy life. And I did. We went everywhere together." He smiles as he looks at a picture of the two of them on the nightstand. She has her arms around him, and they are both smiling. The wind is blowing her hair off to the side, and it's rather remarkable to see their happiness captured so perfectly.

"I don't understand why so many bad things have happened to her. Why is she being left behind?"

He looks up at me with huge blue eyes that demand answers, but I have nothing. So I tell him the truth. "I don't know."

He sighs heavily. "I didn't think you would."

We sit in silence for a few moments, and I ponder what to do. I can't take him with me. He's tied to his body, and besides, the mists refused to come to me in this place. But I can hardly leave him here. He doesn't belong. He was supposed to die long ago, and he knows it. He's out of place. In limbo. How could a mother do this to her own child? She obviously knows about our world, the mechanics of it at least. She must know he's meant to go home. It is not a gift to keep him here this way.

After a time, he interrupts my thoughts. "She's not all bad. You know that, right?" There's a pleading note in his voice, as if I might have some role in deciding her fate. He seems to have a greater understanding of the ramifications of his mother's actions than she does.

I don't answer. I used to think I knew. What she did to Lily, to all those other souls, is unforgivable. But maybe he's right; maybe her love for him means she's not all bad. She doesn't seem like that happy, loving mother in the hallway pictures anymore, but is that person still in there somewhere? Buried deep inside?

"She's not strong enough to deal with another loss. With me going home." His voice catches, and I reach out for his hand on impulse before pulling it back. I can't take him anywhere, and I'm afraid if I make contact, I'll doom him to being a ghost. But this little boy knows he's stronger than his own mother, that she needs him more than he needs her, and the weight of that is breaking my heart. All I can do is sit back and listen to him.

"I wish she would let me go," he whispers. "Is that horrible of me? Wanting to leave my own mother behind?"

If possible, the tiny pieces of my broken heart break even more for him. I kneel down on the floor in front of him, barely resisting the urge to put my hands on his knees. Looking up at him, I can feel the tears pooling in my eyes. This poor boy. He started it all, without even knowing it.

"No, my sweet boy. That doesn't make you horrible. It makes you...well, human. You don't belong here. You know it. I know it. It's just taking your mom a little longer to figure that out."

"She's lost so much already." He says it so quietly that I almost don't hear him.

"Yes, she has," I say, thinking of her very soul and the things she's sacrificed for her chosen path. She's lost more than he knows.

Before we can take the conversation further, I hear a sound in the house. The slamming of a screen door.

"You should go. You shouldn't be here," he says quickly. The sadness in his eyes is replaced by fear, making me wonder what he's seen in this place.

"She will use you. Turn you into something you're not. Think of Nathair. *Go*," he urges.

Think of Nathair. Is that what she did to him? Did she somehow change him into something he wasn't? Force him to join her? Does that possibility make me think more of Nathair or less of Mara? I'm not sure.

I can't help reaching for him, but he pulls away. "Come with me," I beg, knowing he won't.

"I can't. You know I can't. The mists won't come here."

Before I can ask him how he knows that, the bedroom door abruptly opens. I stand, turning to block Shiloh's soul with my body.

But it isn't Mara standing in the doorframe. Nor is it Nathair.

Quietly, the man closes the door behind him and turns to face me.

The shock nearly keeps words from forming. But, eventually, I find my voice. "Webber. What are *you* doing here?"

SEVEN

Penn

I see her. The anger she feels is almost overwhelming. When you combine it with the grief and desperation, I'm almost taken in. Almost. Sympathy threatens to form in my mind, but I push it back. This woman is responsible for trapping eight innocent souls in hell. Eight. One wrongfully trapped soul is far too many. Eight is a tragedy that can't be tolerated, not to mention the massive amount of ghosts on Earth this whole mess created.

I see her driving. Nathair sits next to her in an old pick-up truck. I think it was yellow at one time, but age and rust have made it hard to tell.

"Did you take care of the girl?" Mara asks. There's no empathy in her cold voice. I can feel the love she holds for her own child. But it's clear she holds no affection for this girl she's talking about.

"I did." Nathair shifts in his seat, as if he's uncomfortable. "Mara," he finally says, "why can't we just let them go to heaven after we cut their threads?"

She slams on the brakes in the truck, and Nathair only stops himself from crashing into the dashboard by bracing his body with his long legs.

"You dare to question me? You know there was no *we* when I started this. There was only Shiloh. And if you're not in this for the right reasons, I can do it without you."

Shiloh. Her son. I'm slowly putting the pieces together. This is about Shiloh. I struggle to remember the boy. His thread was terribly short, but that's all I can recall off the top of my head. Suddenly, I have the urge to break away and find Shiloh's thread, but I need to know where they are.

"True, it was harder without you. It wasn't easy to bend the Reapers to my will, but it got me to the heavens…and my memory-erasing spell ensured they were none the wiser. But it was a challenge I mastered as time went on. I can do this without you."

Nathair sits quietly for a moment. But something is bugging him. I can tell from all the sidelong glances he's making at her.

"But why the prison, Mara? They are suffering. You know what happened to Nysa. Isn't there some way we could—?"

She cuts him off. "Nysa got what she deserved. She didn't want to help my Shiloh. She had the audacity to tell me to let him go in peace." She pauses as she makes a turn down a dirt road. "The others…are unfortunate."

"But if we correct it, maybe we can save them."

I can't believe what I'm hearing. He wants to save them. He's not invested in this the same way she is.

"My, my, Nathair. You are a softie, aren't you? In fact, I think your Reaper is showing." She smiles playfully at him and puts her hand suggestively on his knee. "I like this soft side I'm seeing. But no, my sweet. There's nothing I can do for them now. Their threads have been cut early so if they go on to heaven, their threads become…unviable. I found that out the hard way. So they must go to the prison."

"But they'll all just vanish."

"A casualty of war, I'm afraid. A sacrifice I'm willing to make. Aren't you?" She bats her eyelashes up at him and stares at him with her huge green eyes. I want to shout at him. *She's manipulating you, you idiot. Listen to your instincts!* But he wouldn't hear me. I am nothing more than an observer. Once we set a thread's fate in motion, that soul is out of our hands. And Mara is so far out of reach, I fear we may never find her.

Instead of answering her, Nathair turns his attention out the window. I do the same, trying to see down the road. The thick forest makes it hard to grasp exactly where they are, but I can see a log cabin up ahead. A few more moments tells me that's where she's heading. And that must be where Michaela is hidden too.

I pull back from the tapestry abruptly. Shiloh. My eyes dart up Mara's thread until I find where Shiloh's branches off it. It's actually hard to see. As it is expertly woven back into the tapestry, I have to work hard to free it. Once I do, I'm shocked at what has happened to it.

"Horatia. Look at this."

I trace his thread with my finger. It's unnaturally long. It changes from the vibrant blue to a myriad of colors, including what looks like a bit of a sparkler. Is that Kismet? I can't tell for sure. It's woven back into the tapestry, so I can't quite see where it ends now.

"Do you remember this boy?" I ask.

She scrutinizes his thread. "Yes. His thread was shorter than this when I gave it to Webber."

Galenia peers over my shoulder at it. "He was supposed to die from cancer ages ago."

"Indeed."

When I peer into his thread, the boy is lying in bed, inside the home. I can hear voices outside the door. One of them is female. The sound is muffled and hushed, but I recognize it in an instant. *Michaela.*

The urge to go to her is overwhelming. She's so close, but I'm not really there. I try to silently send her strength and encouragement. I*'m coming for you*, I whisper. Yet in some ways, I'm as far from helping her as ever. After all, I can have no effect on the people or events I see through the tapestry.

It's time for us to take our next step, whatever that is.

"I know where she is," I say, pulling away again. Or, at least I think I do. No need to let the others in on my doubts. At least not yet.

"Where?" Horatia demands.

"In some isolated log cabin in the Pacific Northwest."

"Be more specific. Do you have coordinates or anything?" she asks.

"No." I'm starting to feel dumb.

Horatia folds her arms over her chest and looks me up and down. "So how do you plan to extricate her?"

Galenia puts a hand on her sister's shoulder, and she relaxes a bit.

"Same way I figured out where she is. Follow my gut."

EIGHT

Michaela

Webber is breathless as he sinks to the floor just inside of Shiloh's room, leaning his back against the door.

"Who's that?" Shiloh's soul asks. He seems very intrigued by the new soul in his room. "I've never seen someone like him before."

"That's Webber. He's a Spinner. One of the three Fates. He creates those threads that are…" I stop, instantly regretting that I've drawn attention to the very threads the boy's mother is using to anchor him here. "He creates the threads of life."

"Wow! Really? That is so cool! Can you show me?" he asks with the type of wonder only a small child can possess. His eyes are sparkling as he looks at Webber, and it's obvious Webber isn't quite sure what to do. He's clearly not used to this level of admiration. Particularly not considering the way things are going.

He raises his knees and rests his arms on them. "I can't show you right now, kid, but I tell you what, you get to heaven and you can come watch me spin any time you like."

Of course, it's an idle promise—the souls taken to heaven won't ever see the Fates' workroom, but it's the gesture that counts. Shiloh gives him a huge grin. "Deal!" he says.

Webber looks at me, and I can see his confusion beyond the smile he's put on for the boy. His eyes dart to the rope connecting the body on the bed to the soul in the chair, and his expression turns serious. When he realizes what they are, he abruptly rises to his feet.

"What's happening here, Michaela? Who *is* this boy?" he demands, as if the boy's soul weren't right here in front of us.

"This is Shiloh. Mara's son."

"Mara?" he asks. "The human? The one responsible for trapping the souls?"

His eyes are focused on the crudely constructed rope, and it's as if he's forgotten the boy attached to either end. "She's keeping him here? That's what this is about? Saving her son? So many lives—"

I cut him off. Shiloh doesn't need to hear about the ramifications of his mother's actions. I suspect he already knows what she's done, but the reminder will only hurt him. "Webber. What are you doing here?"

He finally takes his eyes away from the rope and looks at me. Smiling smugly, he shrugs. "Isn't it obvious? I'm here to rescue you."

I smile. I can't help it. "I knew you were a gray thread, Webber."

"What's that supposed to mean?"

I go to him and kiss him on the cheek. "It means you're not all bad."

He rubs his cheek where I kissed him and mumbles, "I always kind of liked the darker threads."

I nod, but my response is interrupted by another sound in the house. There are voices, a man and a woman's, followed by the sound of the front door opening and closing.

Shiloh's soul isn't excited anymore. He's terrified. "You have to go. She can't find you here."

Webber puzzles at the boy for a moment. Rather than wait for Webber to come to his own conclusions, I nod and take Webber's hand, trying to give him a sense of urgency. "*I* will come back for you, I promise."

But instead of saying the kind of things a little kid should say, such as, 'You better,' or 'I can't wait,' Shiloh turns sad. "I'm afraid no matter how many times you come back, I'll still be beyond your reach." He sounds a million years old now.

All the urgency to save myself drains when I hear the exhaustion in this child's voice. I let go of Webber and take a step toward Shiloh. "I will build a bridge to you, Shiloh. I promise. Come hell or high water, I will *not* abandon you."

He looks at me, but I can tell he's battling with himself. He feels guilty for hoping that I'll succeed. Despite what she's done, a big part of him doesn't want to leave his mother. I can see the struggle on his face. I smile reassuringly at him, knowing that's all I can do for now, and turn toward the door.

Just as I take a step in Webber's direction, the door flies open, hitting him hard before bouncing back. I freeze in place, knowing exactly who's on the other side. Only one person would open the door with that kind of violence and fury.

Webber is in a heap on the floor, holding up an arm in defense in case the door should swing open again. *Some knight in shining armor.* I shake my head as I look at him, not quite cowering, but not exactly rushing forth to defend me either.

Slowly, the door swings open again. I see her arm first, and then the rest of her steps into view.

"Well. Funny meeting you here," Mara says as she glares at me with such hate that I'm not sure she even remembers how to smile. It's then I know the woman she was died when her son should have.

NINE

Penn

We leave the weaving room in silence just before the work-day is scheduled to start.

The girls wander into the workroom, and I follow them automatically. Webber has yet to arrive, leaving the three of us to our thoughts.

"Did you actually *see* Michaela?" Horatia asks, looking for comfort, or maybe assurance that we're on the right track.

"No. But I know she's in that house."

"How?"

"I heard her. Listen—we find Mara, we find Michaela. Besides, this isn't just about finding Michaela, or freeing Kismet and the other souls. Mara has ruined a lot of lives, and we can stop her."

"And how do you plan to get there? Jump off the edge of the heavens like you did the last time you went to Earth?" Horatia asks. I don't miss the sarcasm in her tone.

"Well, I…" I stammer. Galenia comes to my rescue.

"The mists. Why not use the mists?"

"That would be the simplest solution, but we don't have a Reaper at our disposal…" I trail off, racking my brain to make it work, to fit the pieces together.

"Why don't we head over to the Reapers' wing to see if we can follow one down to Earth?" she suggests. It's not a bad suggestion. Except we might end up across the world from Mara and Michaela.

"Because we have our own work to do," Horatia said, glancing at the door. "Where is Webber?"

He isn't typically late. According to Horatia and Galenia, he tends to show up early to get a head start on the day. You can't fault his work ethic.

"What do you want to do? I can always go alone," I say.

The daggers shooting from Horatia's eyes make me shrink back behind Galenia, who smiles comfortingly at me.

"Did he say he'd be late today?" Galenia asks.

"No."

"Let's go look in his quarters for him," Galenia suggests.

"To what end?" I ask. "So you can get to work? Or so you can invite him to come?" I'm not really on board with either option, to be honest.

They're both silent. "The more time we waste, the further Michaela gets from us. The further *Mara* gets from us."

"Penn," Horatia scolds. "We can't just disappear."

"Why not? It seems like Webber has." To my mind, it's a valid point.

Horatia shrugs. "It's not like we have to go back to hell to look for him. Let's just walk by his room."

"Then what? If he's there, you'll either have to pretend everything's normal, which means you, Galenia, and Webber will have to work today, or we'll have to bring him with us."

"Penn's right," Galenia says with a sigh. "Looking for him seems to be a lose-lose situation. Besides, I can't bear to spend another unproductive day in the workroom. Not when everything's so shaken up."

Horatia lights up. "Penn, you go knock on his door. Galenia and I will hang back so he doesn't see us."

This is basically the worst idea ever. "I don't even want to check on him! Why should I knock on his door?"

"Tell him we're waiting for him, but we're going to leave for the day if he takes much longer. That way he won't think anything of it when we're not here." She's clearly more of a fan of her genius than I am.

Galenia is nodding in agreement, though, and I know I've lost this battle. But if it means we're going to get Michaela, I've won the war.

I take a deep breath before knocking on Webber's door. I've never felt so conflicted in my life. I don't want him to be there, but I also don't want him to be in any real danger. Although it's not something I'd admit to my sister Fates, I do think it's odd that he didn't show up. Webber's never missed a day of work, so why would he start now?

Before I can talk myself out of it, I knock hard on his door. I look down the hall at my sisters, who are peeking around the corner, watching anxiously.

Shifting my weight, I look back at them and shrug.

Horatia waves me on. She wants me to go in.

"No," I whisper. "What if he's busy? Naked or something? No. I'm not going in there. If he doesn't want to answer the door, that's on him."

Horatia approaches fast. "Fine. I will." She reaches for the door, but before she can ruin everything, I open it and go in. She stays just behind the doorframe, out of sight.

To my surprise, the room is empty.

"Happy? He's not here," I say, but I feel just as unhappy as Horatia and Galenia look.

He's not here.

"Where is he?" they ask simultaneously, barely speaking above a whisper.

I sigh. "One lost heavenly being at a time. He's probably just brooding in the observatory. We don't have time to search for him right now. He'll turn up." Although I don't know that for sure—and I'm a little concerned too—I can't let anything keep us from Michaela.

"We need to get Michaela," I add.

I can tell they're more worried than ever, but they both nod.

"Okay, then. Let's see if we can't find our way through the mists."

The workday is now in full swing, so you'd think the Reaper's wing would be teaming with activity, but no one's around when we walk past the glass walls of the naming room.

Honestly, I'm relieved. I have my Keeper's uniform on, but my sisters are a bit conspicuous in their glittering gold robes. We walk silently down the stark white corridors to the golden gate. The gate is mere yards away when someone stops us.

"What do you think *you're* doing?" The words echo down the empty hallway, making us all freeze where we stand—or crouch. Even her steps sound angry. I wish she would quiet down. We're so close. I don't want other Reapers to join her crusade.

Galenia turns and flashes the sweetest smile she can conjure. Her smiles are so irresistible, I find myself smiling along with her.

"You're Fates," the girl says in surprise. "What are *you* doing here?" She's small, much smaller than Michaela, and the long, black-and-white Reaper's gown seems to dwarf her even more.

"We have some business…in the mists. I think it would be best for you to move along," Galenia suggests sweetly. I'm not used to seeing this assertiveness in her. I have to say, I like it.

"Maybe I should get Ryker. He can help you get what you need." Her voice is soft, almost meek. I wonder if she's a friend of Michaela's.

"No, that's not necessary," Horatia bursts in, holding up a hand. "But thank you for the offer," she adds quickly, trying to cover up her urgency.

The Reaper scrutinizes the three of us a little longer. I can only hope she doesn't recognize me. I don't recognize her, so maybe, just maybe, I have that going for me.

"You're Michaela's friends, aren't you? The Fates she's always talking about."

None of us responds. I can see Horatia and Galenia shift their weight as I avoid eye contact. I can't help but notice she used the blanket term of Fates to identify us. She didn't single me out as a Keeper. Does she know who I am?

"Are you trying to help her?"

I peek between my sister Fates for a better look at the Reaper. She's straddling the line between lowering her guard and calling for reinforcements. There will be no middle ground, no scenario in which she just walks away and lets us do our thing without telling anyone. She's either going to help us or report us.

After we spend a few moments suspended in tension, Galenia nods and the Reaper steps forward.

"I'm Miette," she says. "I'm a friend of Michaela's too. How can I help?"

My sister Fates stand there in slack-jawed amazement. This is no time for inaction, so I take a chance and step out from behind them.

"Miette," I say. "Your name sounds familiar. I think I've heard her talk about you." I smile, trying to offer some reassurance to the small Reaper in front of me. "If you really want to help, we could use a guide through the mists," I say, thinking of my most immediate problem.

She glances around nervously. "I'm supposed to be working. Helping the new recruits. I was on my way to the training floor now. If I disappear, they will know something is up. Let me go get them started on a task, and then I'll come meet you outside."

She takes off running before any of us can respond, leaving us standing a few yards from the gold door.

"She seems sweet," Galenia says, still smiling after the small girl.

"How long do you think we should wait out there for her? The Reapers who are coming and going are likely to see us lingering in the clouds," Horatia points out.

"True. But no one else will take us exactly where we need to go," I say, feeling like meeting her was a bit serendipitous. It's bound to work out. Right?

I have absolutely no idea, but I turn and make my way toward the golden door, bringing my sisters with me. The only thing we can do is act and hope for the best.

We wait among the clouds for a long time, or at least what feels like a long time. Horatia and Galenia sit on the steps while I pace around a few yards away. We don't speak. There's nothing to say at the moment. We don't speculate about Webber, Michaela, Kismet, or Andrew. We just wait.

Now that we're standing still again, I can't help but worry about Kismet. Are she and Andrew still locked in that prison in hell, waiting for us to return? But I've made my decision, and I can't look back. Michaela's in an equally dangerous situation, and if we don't save her, we can't save Kismet. Besides, I've already lost so much; I can't bear to lose someone else I care about. I can't lose Michaela. I know it like I know how to spin.

"Do you think Miette got sidetracked? Maybe we should go without her," Horatia suggests, clearly getting antsy by the way her knees are bouncing. "Someone's bound to notice the Fates are all missing. We should get moving before we miss our chance."

"How? How are we going to go on? We haven't seen a single Reaper since we came out here," I snap.

"To be fair, I don't think we've really been out here that long. It only seems that way," Galenia says, ever the peacemaker.

Just as I'm about to rattle off a perfectly witty rebuttal, Miette comes through the door and stays my tongue.

Her sober expression stops my pacing dead in its tracks. "You know where she is, don't you?"

Horatia says, "No."

At the same time, I say, "Yes."

Confusion plays on Miette's face. I can hardly blame her. "I know how to find her," I offer, hoping it's enough not to scare her off.

"And you think she's on Earth?"

"I do."

"And you planned to get there by going through the mists?"

"Yup."

She holds her arms out to me, as if pleading with me to give her more information, or maybe just better information. "What would you have done if I hadn't come along? How did you plan to get through them without a Reaper?"

I shrug. "Luck," I say, not wanting to vocalize our ridiculous plan to follow a Reaper and hope they got us in the proximity of Mara and Michaela.

She frowns at me. She's more serious than Michaela, and I'm not sure how to handle her. If I make her too uncomfortable, she may change her mind about helping us.

"Has that approach worked well for you in the past?" She raises an eyebrow at me, making me shift in place. I wonder again if she knows who I am.

I try a disarming joke. "You're here, aren't you?"

She chuckles quietly, and I let out a sigh of relief. "Point taken. So, where are we going?"

Horatia turns to me. "Yes, where *are* we going?"

Miette looks at me curiously.

"I'm not sure, to be honest. I saw it in the weaving room. Is that enough to go on?"

Miette smiles broadly. "The mists are mysterious. They follow the soul that leads them." She holds out her arm toward the gathering mist. "Lead on."

After we've walked through the mists for a time, Miette breaks the silence.

"You know, Michaela saved me." I start to wonder if I heard her right, but she picks up her explanation before I can press her. "I nearly aligned myself with the wrong crowd. A mistake that would've cost me my job. My life as I know it. She opened my eyes. She didn't even know me at the time, but she offered me a lifeline to the right choice." She's quiet for a moment. "I owe her this."

She turns to me and looks me right in the eye, as if I'm in

charge of Michaela's fate. "Bring her back." It's not a request—it's an order.

I nod firmly, trying to let her know I'm not taking her order lightly.

She doesn't say anything more. Either Miette doesn't want to know our plan or she's too afraid to ask. That's a good thing… because we don't have one. At all. We never progressed past stumbling our way through the mists.

My mind races as we walk through the white expanse of nothingness. What will we find on the other side? Will Mara be there? Nathair? Webber? Michaela? How will we get her back? Perhaps the how doesn't matter. The only thing that matters is that we *will* get her back. We must.

And we will put an end to Mara's reign of terror. A part of me feels very responsible for what she's done. I spun her, for heaven's sake. I set this into motion, intentionally or not. Of course, that thought only leads to darker and darker thoughts as the mists billow up around us.

When the mists finally begin to clear, I slow my pace, not quite ready to face the latest life-or-death challenge.

Miette turns to face us, and I know she's about to leave. "If you fail, I'm not sure how you will get back," she says in a small voice. "I can't wait for you. My little field trip must go un-noticed."

I nod, though the risk we're taking weighs on me. If we don't return soon, it will be disastrous. With three Fates stuck on Earth and one unaccounted for, the birth rate will be at an absolute stand still. Galenia's statement echoes through my mind again. All of this is going to end soon, one way or another.

"Good luck," Miette says. Then she looks me in the eye. "I'm counting on you."

TEN

Michaela

"Shiloh, my sweet baby. I didn't realize you had visitors. I'm going to take good care of them for you, okay? Mommy will be right back."

Mara's son looks at her with his broken heart painted all over his face, and it brings tears to my eyes. But she's not looking at him. She's looking at his body.

Surely, she must know what she's doing to him. She made the rope. She maintains it. She *must* see him. But she's ignoring his soul, his essence, looking only at the boy in the bed. She kisses him gently on the forehead, adjusts his covers, and glances at his heart monitor before stepping away.

And in that one step, she goes from tender mother to ruthless captor in nothing flat. It's frightening. She lunges forward, like she's going to take us by the arms or something, but then she simply holds the door open and gestures for us to leave the room. I look at Webber and he shrugs, as if he doesn't have any other ideas. I suppose it's the thought that counts, but thoughts aren't going to save us.

Nathair is out there waiting for us, and he saves Mara the chore of roughing us up. Grabbing us both by the arm, he jerks us down the hall, tugging us back toward the basement. From over my shoulder, I watch as Mara flashes one last gentle smile at her son's body and shuts the door behind her.

"Nathair. Please. Stop this now. You know the consequences of this path."

"Quiet." He gives me a shove to accentuate his point, but it's half-hearted. He has doubts.

"You've seen what she can do. It's amazing. But this path will end. And I don't want you to be on it when it does. Please, help us. Do the right thing here."

Mara is waiting impatiently by the basement stairs. "That. Is. Enough," she seethes. "The *right* thing is what we're doing for Shiloh, so you can shut your judgmental little trap right now." She probably spoke in a whisper so Shiloh wouldn't hear her, but it only made her sound more menacing. She glares at me, and then nods for Nathair to take us down.

The only sign the Reaper isn't thrilled with her orders is his conflicted expression. It doesn't matter—for now, he's still helping her. Nathair opens the basement door and shoves Webber down in front of him. I get dragged by the wrist. Webber trips several times on the way down the basement stairs, and I can tell he's terrified. He hasn't even seen what this woman can do, but he's literally falling all over himself out of fear of her, Nathair, or maybe the whole situation. I can't tell. To be honest, it *is* overwhelming. I take a deep breath. I will get us out of this. I just hope Webber doesn't do anything desperate or stupid to make our bad situation worse.

Nathair rather unceremoniously shoves us into the small room where I was held captive. Then he steps inside so Mara can follow. I can feel her anger crackling in the room, almost like electricity snapping around us. Her nostrils are flared, her eyes are burning, and she's breathing in short gasps. The demons we encountered in hell scared me less than the sheer force of her rage. And we're cornered with her in a small, dark space.

A quick glance at Webber, who's trying unsuccessfully to hide his terror, tells me I'm completely on my own. Even more so than when I was in the depths of hell.

The human takes another deliberate step into the room, bringing even more of that electric feeling with her. It makes the hair on my arms stand up.

"Who do you think you are, going to see him?" she demands. The barbed words are directed at me, as if she somehow knows I sought him out and Webber just stumbled upon us. "Did you think you could take him from me? After everything I've worked for? That I would bring you into our home so you could ruin everything?

"I know you aren't on board, but Nathair wasn't at first either." She shoots him a seductive look. "He only needed a little persuasion. I intended to persuade you too—I just haven't found your weakness yet. Don't make me regret sparing you."

Her words feel laden with power, and the light in the hallway flickers despite the fact that no one has moved to turn it off. A wicked smile steals across her face.

"Mara, how did you come to be so powerful?" I ask, ignoring her question and trying to stroke her ego a little. Distraction, that's what I need. Time. I need time to form a plan.

"My powers were not so unusual once." She looks down at one hand and rubs the fingers together, making a visible spark. "My mother and grandmother were both witches. I wasn't born with these powers—they came to me through knowledge that was passed down from generation to generation.

So she's a witch? It's been years since I last led a self-proclaimed witch through the mists. Even so, I've never seen a human produce a spark by rubbing their fingers together. And I've never seen anyone vanquish an Archangel period, let alone with a mere touch. I'm in way over my head here, trying desperately to learn to swim.

But Mara doesn't respond to my obvious bafflement. She keeps right on talking, and it's obvious it's been a while since she's spoken to anyone other than Nathair and Shiloh. "My mother died when I was a young girl, and she took my father with her. They said it was a car crash, but I knew better. She couldn't have been killed by something so common. She was a rather unstable soul." Her shrug implies it meant nothing to her.

"Who raised you?" I ask, eager to keep her talking.

"My grandmother." She sighs and looks off into the distance. "She died years ago. Long before I met my husband. She would have loved showing Shiloh her 'parlor tricks' as she called them. Simple magic to wow the children, like pulling a mouse out of her sleeve, or a flower from behind the kid's ear.

"Most of what I learned about *your* world, I learned fairly recently. I traveled all over collecting knowledge from different covens, putting the information together piece by piece. It wasn't easy, traveling with a sick child. His doctors thought I was dooming him to an early death, but it turns out we didn't need them. I've kept Shiloh alive on my own longer than any of them thought he would last.

"Then my dear Nathair came along. That little development has certainly made things easier. I had to convince him to help me, of course, but you'll find I can be very persuasive." She smiles at him. He smiles back, but their expressions are totally different. Hers is cold and full of victory, and his...his is soft, and there is a bit of a wistfulness in his eyes. Does he love her? Something about the way he's looking at her makes me wonder. Did she somehow force him to feel that way? She said he needed persuasion. What exactly does that mean? Her words send a cold shiver down my back.

She keeps talking—it's almost as if she can't stop. "Until recently, the true extent of my skill was theoretical. Those two angels confirmed the magnitude of my abilities."

She gives me a smug look. "You speak of consequences to Nathair. But what authority does God have against someone who shares his capabilities?" She raises her sparking hand a bit.

I gasp involuntarily. "If you honestly believe your powers rival God's, you are already lost." It's a devastating truth, not a threat. But she ignores me.

Shrugging, she shifts gears, veering back into more neutral territory. "I never did teach Shiloh the ways. He wasn't very old when his father died, and I was devastated. All alone, with no one to help me raise this little boy who looked just like his father. In fact, he looks so much like him, it hurt to look at him at first."

My mind is working hard to stay two steps ahead of her, but she's given me so much information to consider that it's hard to stay focused.

"But I love him. I love him with all that I am." Mara turned her gaze back to me, and it was once again hard, cold, and full of hate. "What right do *you* have to him, after everything I've lost? How can you not understand that I *need* him?" Her emotions are swinging around so wildly, it's hard to keep up. "He's all I have left in this world." It comes out dripping with sadness, but I don't trust it. She's clearly manipulative, and though I don't doubt her love for the boy, I definitely doubt her sincerity. It's important to tread lightly.

"Mara, it's not that we don't understand. Death is…difficult to accept," I say carefully.

Mara scoffs, but I keep talking to her, trying to keep my voice as soft and soothing as possible. "But you're causing others the same pain you're trying to avoid. The last thread you cut belonged to a child. A young girl. You stole her from her parents. You haven't solved your problem…you've only diverted it to someone else. Over and over again." I take a step toward her, though every last inch of my body is crying out for me to run away.

Her expression tightens. "I needed to take a child close to Shiloh's age. I thought it might be a more permanent solution." She tilts her head, studying me as I take another step, hoping I can somehow gain the upper hand if I close the distance between us.

"Besides, better them than me." She wears a chilling smile as she says it, and it's hard to resist the urge to shudder.

"Is it, Mara? Because that fate wasn't meant for them. It was meant for Shiloh. You obviously don't believe your actions won't be met with retribution, but I urge you to—"

She cuts me off. "It's not your place to *urge* me to do anything. *I* control his fate now." Finally, she looks over at Webber. "What do you think of that, Spinner?"

Webber doesn't respond, and for that, I'm thankful. How does she know? Must be his gold clothing. The thought gives me an uneasy feeling. What other secrets of my home does this woman know? And how can she use the information against me?

"I've suffered enough losses in my lifetime."

"And you plan to keep doing this until you die? Just cutting thread after thread after thread for the next fifty years?"

"Ah, fifty years? Is that how long I'll be on this Earth? Good to know," she answers, ignoring the larger issue.

All of a sudden, she takes a deep breath and nods to Nathair, who exits the room.

"Don't test me again," she said, staring at us with her burning eyes. "I think you'll both prove rather useful. It'll be particularly handy to have a Spinner around. Maybe I won't have to cut any more threads after all—huh, Reaper? I bet that would make you pretty happy."

Webber tenses. "I can't just make life out of nothing."

Mara laughs out loud. "I'm sorry. I thought that's what Spinners did."

Flustered, he shrugs. "That might be the basic gist of it, but the materials I need are only found in my cauldron. I can't just knit you a sweater and tell you it's made of lives."

She doesn't miss his snark, and the smile melts from her face. "No. I don't suppose you can. Lucky for you, I have time to troubleshoot that small detail. Perhaps Nathair will have some ideas. He spends a great deal of time around your workstation anyway."

Webber steps forward to protest, but I grab his arm, stopping him in his tracks.

Mara smiles. "Don't make me eliminate you both." She turns to leave but stops in the doorway to add one last thing. "You could prove very useful indeed," she says as she slams the metal door home.

And just like that, I'm trapped in the basement again.

ELEVEN

Penn

The mists aren't clearing like they should. They're unusually thick considering how far we've come from where we left Miette.

We walk carefully, not sure of what's in front of us. There are big, looming shapes all around us. Based on the map we saw in Ryker's office, I can only assume they're trees. My feet crunch through the vegetation, but the mists drown out the sound. As we walk, the mists get thicker, not thinner, as if they're bouncing off some object in front of us. But the white vapor is so dense, we can't see what that object might be.

It's almost as if the mists are climbing an invisible, dome-shaped wall stretched out in front of us, and then pouring back off it in waves. What could it mean?

Horatia and Galenia have never been to Earth before, so they probably don't realize this is abnormal. When I look back at them, they seem less focused on the mist than they are on their first real-life experience of a forest. They're looking all around, soaking in all the details. I can't help but smile at their show of appreciation.

"What is it, Penn?" Galenia asks, finally sensing something's off.

"This is odd. The mists usually clear, not gather. Something is blocking them." I nod toward the dome shape in front of us, but it's hard to see it through the murky air.

"What does it mean?" Horatia asks as she holds out a hand, letting the mist pouring off the dome roll over it. It doesn't leave any moisture behind as real fog would. It just passes over her, leaving no trace of itself on her skin.

"Michaela is beyond this...dome or whatever it is. We have to get to the other side," I say, convinced I'm right. There are no alternatives. We have to keep going. We certainly can't get back to the heavens without Miette or Michaela. We need a Reaper to get home, and the one I want is straight ahead. Through the peculiar dome.

"What are you suggesting?" Horatia asks, obviously a bit leery of the situation.

"I think I'm just gonna go through it and see what happens. If it doesn't hurt me, you can follow, okay? If it does, find another way in. You have to save her."

"I don't—" Horatia starts to protest, but I'm already moving forward. Out of the corner of my eye, I see Galenia take her hand in comfort, but I can't afford to stop and consider the consequences of my planned action. I have an idea of who created this. She's bad news, so I don't really expect anything pleasant to come from passing through it. Extinction, imprisonment, torture...they're all possibilities.

Despite that, I put out my right hand, glance back at my sisters for one last smile, and then put one foot in front of the other.

I feel no different at all. No searing pain, nothing that melts my arm, no change in the temperature or texture of the air. I press on, continuing to brace myself for...something. The mist at the edge of the dome is so thick that I can't see anything, not even my hand stretched out in front of me. But I keep making my way toward the interior of the dome, toward Michaela. At least I *think* I'm moving toward her. I can't really tell in all this fog. The only way I can ensure I'm moving in a straight line is to literally put one foot in front of the other, walking heel to toe, heel to toe. It's slow, but it makes me feel better about where I'm going.

And then, rather suddenly, the mists clear. I find myself in a beautiful old forest with redwoods that seem to stretch past the sky. Some of them tower so high, I can't even see the tops from where I stand.

I made it through and nothing happened to me. Nothing at all. This is the first thing that's felt easy in a long time. All at once, I'm filled with this odd mix of joy and dread. We've finally had a victory, but at what cost? I let out a hysterical laugh, and it comes out like a bark.

"Penn?" Horatia calls nervously, and I realize that I haven't checked in with my sisters. They probably can't even see me anymore. I turn around quickly, finding myself facing one of the most bizarre things I've ever seen. It's a solid wall of mist, climbing up and bending in toward me. But it's completely flat on this side, as if someone cut through the mists with a sharp knife.

"I'm okay. Come on through," I say as I marvel at the phenomenon.

Galenia stumbles through as if she's been pushed, followed quickly by Horatia, who leaps through and lands gracefully.

They gasp in unison as they take in the expansive forest around us. The sky is only visible in bright patches between the high branches of the canopy. Birds and squirrels call to each other, creating a soothing symphony of sound.

"Wow," Galenia breathes.

"It's no wonder you love it here," Horatia says.

"I've never been here before, Ratia," I point out.

She promptly smacks me on the arm. "On Earth, you ungrateful wretch."

The mists disperse abruptly, cutting my laughter short. Now that my sisters are free of them, they just disappear. There goes our easy path home.

"What's happening here, Penn?" Galenia asks, her voice a mix of fear and amazement.

"I think Mara may be keeping unwanted Reapers out." It's the only thing I can think of. If she's keeping her son here unnaturally, keeping Reapers at bay would be job number one.

My sisters circle around and take in the rest of the forest in awe. We start a long walk through the wilderness, too taken by its beauty to worry that Michaela wasn't waiting for us on the other side of the dome.

We've walked for miles. Or at least, that's what it feels like. I find myself thinking of my very first trip to Earth when I landed smack dab in the middle of a swamp. "Hey, at least we're not trudging through some swamp in Florida right now," I say. Galenia and Horatia look at me as if I have two heads. Of course, they've never been in a swamp before. "Believe me, it's no cake walk."

"And this is?" Horatia says. There are sticks, moss, and dead leaves caught in her gold robe, and her hair is getting wilder by the moment as it gets snagged on tree branches and bushes.

Galenia, however, is walking effortlessly through this wilderness, and she even has a sprig of something green tucked behind her ear. She looks so at home, I wouldn't be surprised if a bird swept down and landed on her hand.

"I like it," she says with a smile.

"Clearly," I say, smirking at her.

"Oh, sure. Mother Nature here is totally at ease," Horatia says, plucking a twig out of her hair. "Where are we? And why didn't Miette get us a little closer to Michaela?"

Horatia's questions bring my own to the surface. Where was the welcoming committee? If the dome is protecting something, shouldn't it be more heavily guarded? Maybe that was just the outer layer of defense, and the real fun lies ahead.

"I don't know," I say. "I think it had something to do with that dome. It must be protecting Shiloh."

"Her son," Horatia says.

"That's what this is all about. She's stealing other people's threads to keep him here." They've probably figured it out too,

60

at least mostly, but this is the first time any of us have said it out loud. Her crimes sound even worse that way. Mara is killing others to keep her son on Earth. The suffering on both sides of this situation must be immense. I can see no gain for anyone.

Truth be told, I'm tired of asking questions and making guesses. I feel worn down by all of it. Kismet, Andrew, the surprises, the tapestry, the prison of lost souls. My whole life has taken on the curve of a question mark.

As we walk through the woods, I can only hope that it all ends here.

TWELVE

Michaela

Once the door slams home, we sit in the darkness for a few moments. They didn't bother to bind us this time. Maybe they figured we'd just get out of the restraints anyway. Who knows? But it's just as dark as it was before. There isn't even a naked bulb in the room; the only light source is on the other side of the huge, metal door.

"We have to get out of here," Webber says.

"I know," I say, wanting to pace, but not wanting to crash into him or anything else. So I stand still.

"Where's the door?" he asks. I notice his voice is coming from my left. He was right in front of me before.

"Be careful moving around. I don't want you to get hurt." Meaning *I'm not in the mood to get stepped on, so watch it.*

"I'm familiar with being trapped in a dark room, Michaela. Thank you," he snaps.

His comment stings enough to make me flinch. We had to leave him in a room like this in hell, and I'm certain he'll never let us forget. Maybe we don't deserve to forget. I don't really feel like saying anything, so I don't answer his question. He'll find the door.

I can tell when he does. I hear his hands pawing at it, searching for a weakness.

Escape. He's so focused on it. He didn't come here for Mara. He came here for me. But I know we can't just leave her to her own devices. If we do, more people will die before their time. It won't stop until she does. Shiloh helped me see that. I need to take her back to the heavens so she can meet with justice.

The thought overwhelms me. I know Webber won't help me with that, but how can I hope to accomplish such an enormous task without assistance? I shake my head in the darkness. These are worries for my future self. Right now, I have to figure out how to get out of this basement yet again.

"There's a window in the door. It slides to the left," I say, barely above a whisper. I'm still a bit wounded by his barb, but he doesn't seem to pick up on my tone. He keeps scraping at the metal door.

I take slow, measured steps forward, not wanting to crash face-first into the post that I know is somewhere in the middle of the room.

I reach Webber before I get to the door. He fumbles in surprise and steps on my foot, making me yelp. "Sorry," he says as he moves away.

"It's just a good thing the Fates don't wear big, heavy boots," I say, wanting to rub my toes all the same. Webber isn't heavy, but he's as solid and muscular as most male heavenly beings. My black-and-white flats did little to protect me.

As soon as my toes stop throbbing, I find the window and try to pry it open, the same way I did before.

This time, it doesn't budge.

I rub my hands on my dress and then try again, this time with more fervor. It still doesn't move. In fact, the longer I hold my hands against the window, the warmer they get. I keep pushing. The heat grows, but it happens so slowly that it takes me a while to realize I'm being burned. My hands are probably red by the time I pull them away, but the darkness reveals nothing.

I kick at the ground. I can tell we're not far from dirt. If we could just get through the foundation layer and dig our way out…

With what? All we have is our bare hands.

I listen for Webber, but he's silent. He's stopped moving around and must've settled down somewhere in the darkness.

"Webber?"

"I'm still here," he says, his voice small and filled with regret.

I don't respond. I sit down with my back against the door and stare into the darkness. Now what?

"Have you been down here before?" he asks, his voice slicing through the darkness.

"Yes. This is where she brought me after…Lily." I don't elaborate, and he doesn't ask. I can't think about that little girl right now, not when she might be in that horrible prison with Andrew and Kismet. It will make me want to crumple into a ball on the floor and let the darkness swallow me forever.

But Webber doesn't care about Lily, at least not right now. He cares about getting out of here. "Judging by Mara's surprise when she saw you in the boy's room, I assume she didn't just let you out. Did you use the window to escape?"

"I did. There's a bolt on the outside that can be reached from the open window."

"Why do you think it won't open now?" he asks.

"I think she did something to it. Bewitched it. Isn't that what they call it?"

"I don't really know. I've never met a witch before."

He doesn't speak anymore, and neither do I. But I know this isn't the end. I'm still here, and as long as I am, I'll keep fighting. I just need to be patient and wait for the next opportunity.

"She will come back for us," I say. "Or maybe it will be Nathair. When that happens, we need to be ready."

"Ready how?" he asks.

"Ready to escape. Ready to win."

———

Our plan is simple. We will sit and wait on either side of the door, and the moment it opens, we will take one or both of them by surprise. Mara is powerful but slight. I think we can handle her *if* we catch her off guard, before she can summon her powers. Nathair is another matter, but it won't help to fret.

We have nothing. No weapons or tools, only ourselves—our hands, our bodies, and our minds.

"We can do this," I tell Webber, suddenly feeling certain of that. "We *must* do this."

"Or what, Michaela? What do you imagine will happen if we don't escape?"

"She will destroy the world, bit by bit." I say it quietly, but the gravity of the words echoes in my mind. Never have I met a human who so earnestly believes she is more powerful than God. There is no precedent for this, no easy path ahead. The destruction of one or the other seems inevitable.

That means failure is truly not an option. I've heard the humans say that before. For their sake, I hope they're right.

Webber and I are in our positions next to the door, so close we could probably touch. But I don't reach out to him. Despite the fact that he came here to rescue me, he's not a kindred spirit like Penn. Nervous energy pours off him, and I have no idea if he will cooperate when the time comes. I can only hope that he does. Or that I can handle the problem if he doesn't.

"Webber, can I ask you something?"

"You just did, so I'm quite confident you can." If Penn had said that exact thing, I would've laughed and swatted him, but coming from Webber, it feels like a barb. I don't know why.

"Why did you come?"

He doesn't answer me, and silence stretches out between us for what feels like years. Centuries. Civilizations rise and fall in the time he takes to speak again.

"I had to."

"Did someone force you?" I ask, trying to think of who would volunteer the world's worst Spinner to rescue a wayward Reaper. Why didn't they send another Reaper? Ryker could have even come himself.

"No. No one made me. I found Mara's thread in the tapestry, and I saw you with her. I went to Ryker, and he guided me here. It wasn't easy to find you, you know. I had to watch Mara for quite a while." He shifts in the darkness, and I imagine him shrugging. As if that explains everything.

"And trudging through the wilderness alone isn't exactly my cup of tea," he says, as if I'm supposed to be grateful for my botched rescue.

The mention of Ryker is shocking. The head Reaper knows where I am? Why didn't he come with Webber? Why would he trust him with such an important mission? "But why? You're... well...terrible at rescue efforts. You remember what happened in hell, right?" I say, throwing caution to the wind.

"A stupid demon abused his power and threw me into a cell. How is that my fault?"

"That's one way to look at it," I say slowly.

"Well, how would *you* look at it?" he asks, his voice rising, defensive. Accusatory.

"Another way to look at it is that you overreacted to something he said and endangered everyone who actually cares about you." My voice matches his own note for note, my irritation plain.

I hear him let out a long sigh, as if he feels defeated. "That's another way of looking at it, yes."

"So, that being said, why did you come here?" I push.

"I told you why."

"'I had to' is not an answer." Despite the fact that he can't see me, I put air quotes around his words. It's so dark that I can't even see my hands doing it.

"That's your opinion." His tone reveals nothing.

I take a deep breath, trying to regain sympathy for this fellow prisoner in the darkness. He did come here for me. I've seen flashes of goodness in him. Not much, but it's there. I hold onto it for dear life.

"Why did you *have* to?"

"Because I don't like who I am." The words shock me. So much so, I have to fight the urge to ask him to repeat himself. I don't think I've ever heard a heavenly being say something like that. Most of us are a bit…well, perfect for lack of a better word. We're different, but we tend not to see our differences as flaws.

"Then why do you act the way you do? Why do you continuously jab at Penn?" I should be understanding and soothing right now. That's what he needs. But the questions just flow out of me.

"It's not all that simple, you know," he shouts at me. The sudden volume in the small space startles me. I sit silent for a moment, letting him cool down.

"I wasn't always like this," he continued in a more subdued voice. "I enjoyed weaving. I was good at it too. But I kept hearing the gossip about Penn. He was totally idolized. He was a born Spinner, they used to say. Like he was some kind of god. But it got me to thinking. Isn't being a Spinner the closest a heavenly being can get to God? They make the threads—I only wove them into the tapestry. It made me want to try harder and do better. After all, why would I just accept that Penn's better than I am?"

My voice leaves me for a few heartbeats. What is with these grey threads and wanting to be like God? "I…Penn isn't *better* than you, at least not in that sense. Is he a more skilled Spinner? Yes. But he isn't a worthier soul. Surely, you must understand that, Webber."

When he doesn't respond right away, I press on. "Penn was always groomed to be a Fate, Webber, just like you were groomed to be an excellent Weaver." I'm not sure I understand his feeling of inadequacy. It's totally irrational. The role of the Weaver is just as important—as *crucial*—as that of the Fates.

Rather than respond, he continues as if I said nothing at all. "I should've been content. I was happy with my life until Penn showed up. And seeing the three of them working so flawlessly together… Well, it wasn't something I could ever be included in. The jealousy consumed me. Everything became about being better than he was. Proving myself. But it was a contest he always won… Until Kismet.

"I knew I had something special when I couldn't get her

to meld into the tapestry. No matter what I did with her, she stood out. She was the most beautiful thread I'd ever seen. Michaela, she was more than one in a million. She was one in infinity. When I saw him staring at her thread in the weaving room, obsessing over her, I knew she'd be my in—my way to show everyone once and for all that I was better. All I had to do was bide my time.

"And it didn't take as long as I thought it would. He slipped up, and I was there to take his place. But the reality turned out to be…" He trailed off. I wasn't sure he was going to finish the sentence, but before I could speak, he picked it back up again. "Well, it wasn't easy. I was—" He swallowed hard. "I was wrong. I was a good Weaver. Some might even say exceptional. But that didn't make me a Spinner. I didn't innately know what I was doing like Penn did. I wasn't made to spin. I was made to weave. But after all the effort I poured into getting the job, I felt committed to it. I had to prevail, to show everyone all the things I'd said for years and years were true."

"Why? Why not just quietly go back to weaving? Be the bigger soul?" I asked.

"I couldn't just accept failure, Michaela."

"Why is succeeding as a Weaver automatically a failure?"

"Because I wasn't a Weaver anymore. I was a Spinner. I *am* a Spinner."

"You can be anything you want. And as a Spinner, you're doing more harm than good. Why didn't you say something? I think everyone would've been happier. Even you."

"I just couldn't, okay? You don't understand," he snaps.

"You're right. I don't. I don't have that much pride. I've seen what it does to humans. It's dangerous. It often leads them to the black gate when it goes unchecked." I didn't intend to sound so self-righteous, but it certainly came out that way. "What I mean is, well…" I sputter a bit.

"What you mean is I'm selfish." I hear a clunk. I imagine he let his head fall back against the cinder block wall behind him, but I'm really not sure.

I don't respond. There's no point. He *is* selfish. It's the quality that grates on all of us. And here he is now, trying to save himself by saving me.

"Is that why Ryker brought you here and then left? So you could redeem yourself?" I ask, trying to fit the pieces together.

"You'd have to ask him why he didn't come with me. I assumed he had other things to do. We didn't talk much on our walk through the mists. He did say he always liked gray threads." He paused. "The man has a flare for the dramatic. Before he left, he also said, 'Don't waste this chance at your redemption, Spinner.'"

So, Ryker had at least a little faith that Webber would succeed. But sitting in this dark basement, across from my assigned savior, it's not much comfort. For the first time ever, I find myself questioning the judgment of my superiors.

After what feels like another eternity of silence, we hear movement outside the door. I stand and hiss at Webber. He shuffles around, and I can only hope he's standing too. We need to pounce on whoever is on the other side of that door.

The lock screeches as it slides open with agonizing slowness, almost as if the person on the other side is struggling with it.

"Something isn't right," I whisper as the door swings open. Webber springs, but I hold back.

The light streams into our little room. Once my eyes adjust, I see he's got a hold of Shiloh.

I rush over to them, growling at Webber, "It's Shiloh, you idiot." He lets the boy go and gives him an apologetic shrug.

As Shiloh straightens his t-shirt, I notice something remarkable. He's complete. This is neither his empty body nor his wandering soul. It's him. Whole.

"What happened?" I ask, concerned by the thought of what his mother might have done to bring about this miracle.

"Nothing. Sometimes, I can come back to my body if I want. Mom likes me to talk to her every once in a while. Not about what she's doing, of course. She gets upset when I talk about that."

He doesn't elaborate, and I don't ask him to. His tone turning urgent, he says, "I can't stay long. It takes a lot of energy to walk around, and she'll know I helped you if I can't talk to her."

His face is gaunt, and his legs don't look like they should support his body. His clothes hang off him, and he sort of shuffles out of our way.

"Webber, carry him back upstairs." I still have no idea what would happen if I touch him. It's not a risk I'm willing to take.

"Don't worry about me. Just go," Shiloh urges as he sinks down to sit on the step nearest to us.

"Webber," I urge. For once, he doesn't argue. He scoops the boy effortlessly into his arms and starts up the stairs.

"You can let go, Shiloh. Save your strength for your mother," I urge. I don't want this poor boy to suffer any more in this life.

"Mom and Nathair left a little while ago," he gasps out. "You should have time to get out. But not much. You need to move," he urges.

Webber reaches the top of the stairs and rounds the corner to the boy's room.

When I follow them into the bedroom, Webber is placing him gently back in his bed.

"I thank you for your sacrifice," I say to the boy's trapped soul. "I will come back for you."

"It doesn't matter. I don't matter. Not in the grand scheme of things. I know that," his soul says as he sits up in the bed, leaving his body behind. He swings his legs over the edge.

"You still deserve peace. Everyone does." I look at Webber, who's already standing in the doorway, ready to go.

"Maybe," Shiloh says, his eyes following mine. "But it's their choice to take what's in front of them. Or not."

THIRTEEN

Penn

We keep walking for miles. For ages. A brooding silence has fallen on our small group, and we stopped paying attention to the scenery long ago. I'm not even going in any particular direction. I'm just putting one foot in front of the other, hoping it's bringing me closer to her rather than farther away.

"Do you think we should turn back? Reevaluate?" Horatia asks. I can tell she's not a fan of the aimless wandering. She needs a plan. Anxiety hangs around her like a cloud.

"I'm not sure," I say, not wanting to speculate at the moment. I can't shake the nagging feeling that Michaela is close. We're going to find her if we just keep going. But that notion sounds ridiculous, even to me.

Just when I'm about to give in to Horatia's request to turn back, the woods start to thin, revealing the first sign of civilization we've seen in hours. We're at the edge of a clearing in front of a medium-sized log house. I smile to myself, somehow knowing Michaela is inside.

───────

We hide at the edge of the woods for a bit, trying to decide what to do.

"Why would a human want to live out here? So isolated?" Galenia asks.

"Probably because they're hiding something."

"Like kidnapped Reapers?" Horatia finishes for me.

I stare at the home. It's probably about fifty yards away, surrounded by green grass, and there are more trees beyond. We're standing on one side of it. I can't see a road leading to it from here, but there must be some way to get in and out.

"If this *is* Mara's home, she needs privacy for whatever she's doing, and she's got it." We're so far from the house, there's no way Mara can hear me, but I find myself whispering nonetheless. She's a powerful woman, and I don't yet know the limits of her power. I'd rather not test her before we even get into the house.

We circle the cabin twice, moving slowly along the edge of the woods as we scope it out, trying to find the best possible entry point. Several minutes pass this way, but there's still no movement around the house. It's hard to see if anything's going on inside from this distance, but one thing's undeniable—no one goes in, and no one comes out.

There is a very long, poorly maintained, and empty dirt driveway. From this vantage point, I can't see the road it connects to, but something tells me it's probably not in any better shape. A porch stretches across the entire front of the house. The sides of the home are relatively bare, with windows here and there, but there's another porch in the back, along with a few chairs, a swing set, and what looks like a neglected tree fort at the edge of the clearing. By the looks of things, Shiloh hasn't been outside in a very long time.

Rather than circle the property a third time, we hunker down around one of the corners, which gives us a good view of the driveway and the side of the house. The best point of entry looks to be around the back. Of course, I can't be sure until we can get a little closer and see what—if anything—is going on inside.

"Perhaps we should take a friendly approach," Galenia

suggests. "You know what the humans say. Sometimes honey catches more flies."

I can't help but laugh. The image of us going to the front door and knocking is just comical to me. "And do what? Knock on the door and ask Mara if she happens to have a Reaper—maybe two—and a wayward Fate in her company?"

Galenia frowns at me. "I'm sorry," I say, putting an arm around her. "I just thought it was funny."

"I wasn't trying to be funny."

Horatia comes to my rescue. "I think a stealthier approach is needed here, Galenia. I'm sorry. There are too many unknowns for us to just reveal ourselves. Surprise is probably our biggest advantage right now."

Gratitude washes over me. At least Horatia and I are on the same page, for the moment anyway.

"Why don't we get a little closer?" Horatia continues. "We don't have to go charging in like the cavalry, but we can peek through the windows, get a feel for who is home, and see if there are any easy ways in. Maybe we can slip in and out without being seen at all."

"Maybe we don't want to get in and out quickly," I say, staring at the cabin. The knowledge that a mere fifty yards stands between one of my dearest friends and me is almost painful.

"Why wouldn't we?" Horatia asks cautiously, clearly ready to change her allegiance at any moment.

"If this is Mara's home, we need to figure out a way to capture her. It's the only way to end this for good. But we can't forget that Nathair is likely with her. When I was watching them in her thread, they seemed...close. Strangely close."

They both shift their weight, the leaves crunching beneath their feet as they consider my words. It's like I've placed a huge obstacle in our path by uttering the truth out loud. The truth is supposed to set you free, right? So why do I feel so weighed down?

Ever since I peered into her thread and saw her at this house on Earth, I knew it would come to this. But now that I've said it out loud in her yard, it's somehow more real. And more daunting.

"They will make things challenging," I whisper.

"Challenging is one way to put it," Horatia agrees.

Galenia remains silent as she watches the house.

A few heartbeats later, I'm starting to think we're just going to sit in the woods forever, waiting for Michaela to come out herself.

"She's in there. I know it," Galenia says, startling both Horatia and me. "Let's go." Without another word, she pushes past Horatia and me and slinks toward the side of the house. She seems like such a quiet and subtle Fate, but even after all these centuries, she can still surprise me.

We hurry to catch up to her, silently approaching the log cabin.

FOURTEEN

Michaela

We're in the kitchen. There's a door along the back wall that leads outside. Or at least it appears to. Webber is bent on going out. But I'm delaying. We need to stop Mara.

"I should've asked him how long he thought she'd be gone," I say as I come to a stop in the kitchen doorway, blocking it. It's very yellow in here. I imagine she was trying to make it feel sunny. She must've painted it at a happier time in her life. Maybe she and her husband did it together. The thought makes me smile, but it quickly fades as I think about all she's lost. The fact that the losses that lay ahead of her are her own fault only makes it worse.

"Why? She isn't here now, so let's go. We might not get another chance."

"Webber…" I hesitate, and he turns to look at me, horror on his face.

"Michaela, I came here for you, and I'm not leaving without you. We have to go *now*." He reaches out a hand for me, beckoning me to come with him.

"We need—"

He cuts me off. "We can't bring the boy. Someone else can

75

come back for him, okay? Send one of your friends after him. Let's get out of danger first. Then we'll send others who are more equipped to deal with this situation."

"More equipped?" I argue. "Who's more equipped to deal with her than two Archangels? She vanquished them with a touch, Webber. A touch!"

"*Not us*," he shouts.

I shoot him a look, imploring him to lower his voice. "Then who?"

"Anyone else, Michaela! *Please*, just come on." He's actually begging me. I can see the desperation in his eyes. He doesn't want to do this. All he wanted to do was rescue me, and he's so close to doing that, but he can see the opportunity slipping away from him. I should probably just let him take me back so he can check his box for redemption. But I can't leave here without her. Leaving Shiloh behind will be hard enough.

"Webber, just go. I'll meet you outside, okay?"

"What?" He hesitates, and I can tell he's considering it. His hand is already on the doorknob. But instead of turning it, he says, "If it means that much to you, go back and get the kid, okay? If it's that or you're not coming, then fine. But hurry up. We don't have a lot of time before she comes back."

He glances around, as if speaking about her will make her materialize in front of us. Frankly, I wouldn't put it past her. Her powers are extensive, diverse, and I still don't fully understand them. I'm not sure I ever will, or that I even want to.

"Webber, this isn't about Shiloh. At least, not right now. At any rate, I can't bring him home. The mists won't answer my call here." It's not something I wanted to admit, but there it is.

"I bet it has something to do with the dome," he says, almost to himself.

"Dome?"

"What?" He looks up at me. "Oh yeah, there's this dome shape around the house. Took me forever to walk here. The mists wouldn't go past it, so Ryker got me as close as he could. I bet that's why you can't call the mists in here. But I bet the boy would be able to go home if you carry him out to them. Just go

76

get him. I'll wait for you here."

"What power could she be using to keep the mists at bay?" I wonder aloud. But Webber doesn't have the answer. After a second, I shake my head. "Please, Webber, just go. How about I meet you at the edges of the mist? Tell me how to find the dome, and I'll meet you there as soon as I can."

He sighs. "Michaela, don't do this. I came all this way."

"For what, Webber? For me? Or for you?" I ask, not to hurt him, but because it's true.

His face falls, and I know my words sting. I expect him to fire a quip back at me in true Webber form, but his shoulders hunch over a bit as he turns and leaves the room, heading outside.

I breathe a sigh of relief, but then immediately feel guilty for it. I hurt him. Deeply. And I'm almost glad I did. It got him to leave. I shake my head, trying to remind myself it's a problem for another day. Something I can work out with him after everything has been resolved.

Slipping out of the kitchen, I pad softly past Shiloh's room. I don't want him to know I'm still poking around the house, looking for anything that will reveal the key to Mara's powers. Everyone has weaknesses, right? But it will only upset the boy to think he might have wasted his limited energy on saving us. The hall branches off into a few other rooms, and I peek into the one nearest Shiloh's.

It's a bathroom, and it's stocked to the gills with medical supplies. Pills, chemicals, gauze, tubes—everything you could possibly want to keep a person alive is lining the vanity, inside the medicine cabinet, and under the sink. I catch myself in the mirror and look at my reflection.

I look frazzled and tired. My hair is out of place, and my dress is definitely worse for the wear after sitting in that basement and being dragged all over creation. The white on it has become more of a dingy gray color. Sighing, I frown at myself before returning my attention to all the implements needed to keep Shiloh alive. That depresses me far more than my appearance.

Deciding I've had enough, I return to the hallway. It dumps out in the front of the house, where a large living room runs the entire length of the home. Mara has a television and couch set up on one side, and three walls of books line the other.

I'm drawn to the books, wanting to know more about where she came from and how her mind works.

Scanning the titles, I see books on everything from witchcraft to the afterlife and the heavens. All are human authors. I'm overwhelmed by curiosity, so I pull out the volume on the afterlife. It's by a woman I reaped not too long ago. She and I had a good laugh over her theories when she saw what it was really like. I smile as I flip through the book. They're pleasant ideas, with one or two notes of truth peppered throughout. Humans have always believed in ghosts, and she correctly theorizes that they exist, but she also speculates that everyone will be a ghost before they "go into the light."

I return the volume to the shelf, searching for more clues. The books on her craft intimidate me, so I skip them. There's too much in them for me to learn anything useful in the few moments I have to look. And what I find in them may frighten me enough to lessen my odds of defeating her. No, I don't need the details of her craft. I need more than that. I need the details of her Achilles' heel.

One other thing stands out to me as I continue my search. Most of the self-proclaimed witches I've met in the past have a healthy respect for the dark side of their craft. Demons, some would call them. The underworld, others would say. But Mara has nothing about hell, demons, or the dark arts. I can't help but be intrigued by that. It's almost as if she's deliberately ignoring the possible consequences of her actions.

I run my fingers along the spines of the books as I walk past the shelves, desperately searching for some sign of weakness in her. But a sudden sound disrupts my search. A cry, just outside the window.

I stop dead in my tracks. I can't make out what he's saying, but I can definitely tell it's Webber. And he sounds panicked.

I rush to the front door and open it carefully, not sure exactly what I'm going to find out there. All I know is that it can't be good.

Webber is standing in the grass, halfway between the house and a line of trees. From this angle, I can only see him, not who he's yelling at. He has his side to me, and he doesn't look over when I slip out of the house. I crouch down, trying to stay hidden behind the porch railing. Conflict rages inside me—should I reveal myself? He seems like he's in distress. His feet are planted firmly in the grass, almost in a defensive stance, and his hands are out in front of him, but it's clear he's not trying to surrender. He's ready for a fight.

"Michaela was right!" he shouts. "You won't stop, will you? You'll never stop. Until we stop you."

I hear a woman's laugh. But it isn't joyful. It's malicious.

Mara. My heart sinks.

"Archangels couldn't stop me, but you think you can? This isn't an episode of *Scooby Doo*, Spinner." The hate in her voice sucks the fun out of her joke. She's impatient, not to mention irritated by the unexpected challenge he's giving her.

Webber glances nervously at the house, and that's when I realize what he's doing. He's delaying her. He's keeping her out of the house to give me a chance to escape. I can't believe it. This selfish Fate is risking his own existence to save me. I want to cry, hug him, and slap him all at the same time. Can't he see she's dangerous? Of course he can, and that's why he's giving me the chance to escape. My emotions war with themselves viciously as I crouch there and watch him.

"Of course we will stop you. And if we don't, someone else will. Evil doesn't prevail. Ever. Or did you miss that memo?"

"And that's where we will agree to disagree," she says. I hear the grass crunching, as if she's walking toward him. Webber takes a step back in defense, but she advances on him until I can see her.

Where is Nathair? I wonder, scanning the grass. She never goes anywhere without him, so I know full well he's lurking somewhere.

"You see, this isn't an issue of good and evil, right or wrong, black or white. This is simply a mother trying to keep what's hers—nothing more, nothing less. You've taken it among yourselves to make it a moral issue. Really, I'm owed his life after everything else you've taken from me." She says it with such conviction that I know she believes it. It's astounding how someone's truth can be a total lie.

She's closing the gap between them. She could touch him at this point if she wanted to.

Enough, I think. I can't let this go on any longer. I need to help him. But something stays my feet. He gave me this opportunity to escape. If I go to him, I'll be throwing his sacrifice away. But does he really need to sacrifice himself?

I sigh impatiently with myself. This indecision isn't helping anyone but Mara. I know one thing is true: I won't be able to live with myself if I leave him, knowing I willingly abandoned him to her.

Just as I'm about to step off the porch, I think I see something out of the corner of my eye. *Penn?* The shock causes me to take a half step back and stare off to the side of the house. He doesn't appear again.

The logical voice tells me that I must've imagined him. I want him here, so my mind summoned him up. That's all. But my heart wishes that isn't true.

"Tell me something, Spinner. What did you hope to accomplish by coming here?" she asks, giving me enough time to stand up. If she glances over here, she will see me. I straighten my back and start to walk toward him. I will stop this. Now. For good. The determination I feel leaves no room for doubt as I reach the steps and descend to the gravel path.

"I intended to rescue Michaela and return to the heavens. That's it," he answers truthfully.

She laughs. "If you have no grandiose plan to stop the villain of your story, what are you doing out here without your dear Reaper?" She's putting the pieces together. Her eyes narrow on him.

I'm watching her as I step into the grass and start walking toward Webber, skirting the porch, staying close to the house.

"You're out here while she's inside, alone, with—" She stops suddenly and turns to run into the house.

That's the moment she sees me. I glance nervously at Webber as her hands fly into the air.

"Even if you eliminate me here, Mara," I shout. "You can't win this. There is no scenario where you win. In fact, the further you take this, the more loss there will be."

"I already have a Reaper. I don't need one who's going to cause me this much trouble."

I brace myself and say a silent prayer that there's somewhere for my innocent soul to go, even though my heart knows there isn't. Heaven is for human souls. Heavenly beings are made to last forever. If we're destroyed, we're gone for good.

Time slows down. Each heartbeat is another movement. I see Webber just a few yards away from me. I see Mara raise her hands in my direction. Then something puzzling happens. Webber is in front of me, screaming. His hands are on me. He's pushing me down. He's on top of me.

A thunderclap so loud it deafens me echoes through the forest around the house. Instinctively, I freeze and bring my hands to my ears, although it's much too late for that.

When I finally feel like I can open my eyes, I can't see anything but white. *I'm blind*, I think. Panic rises like bile in the back of my throat. I blink continuously, and objects start to take shape in front of me. But one thing is noticeably missing.

Webber. I can't breathe. *Webber.* He's gone. There's nothing left of him at all. Not even a shoe left behind, like what led us to him in hell. Nothing. Just like those Archangels.

There are hands on me, dragging me through the grass. But all I can make out are fuzzy shapes and a few colors as my sight slowly returns.

Finally, my lungs fill with a huge breath. Just as I'm about to let it back out as the loudest scream I can muster, someone claps a hand over my mouth and turns me to face him.

Penn.

FIFTEEN

Penn

I don't release Michaela once she sees me. I don't trust her to stay quiet. Mara is too close. What she's done is too fresh.

"Damn it. I could've used him," Mara says. "Oh well. At least we don't have to worry about either of them now. Come on." I hear her footfalls crunching down the gravel walkway. It takes every ounce of control in my possession to stay put as I hear her coming closer to us.

As quietly as I can, I drag Michaela down behind the porch on the other side of the house. Mara walks up to the front stoop, and then slips into the house. We can hear her moving around inside for a while before the commotion settles down. Finally, I feel safe enough to grab Michaela by the hand and make a flat-out run for the woods.

Horatia and Galenia are already there. When I saw the showdown happening, I told them to run for cover. I darted out onto the lawn just before Mara struck Webber, and was able to feel my way back behind the house before that blinding light died down. By then, no one was there, leaving Mara to assume she got both of them. Or so I hoped.

I thought I could help them. But Webber…

What the hell was he doing here anyway? Why wasn't he in the heavens? Did I honestly just see him sacrifice himself for Michaela? That's so out of character for him it's hard for me to wrap my mind around what just happened, even though I saw it unfold in front of me as plain as the nose on my face.

I can hear Michaela's ragged breaths behind me as we run, and I grip her hand tightly, hoping it's enough to help her keep it together until we reach the cover of the woods. With Mara in the house, I'm not foolish enough to think we're safe out here, but we're safer than we were on the porch, that's for sure.

Once we are deep into the woods, I finally let her go. She collapses, and I can see the sob wanting to get out.

"Michaela, please. We need to be quiet."

Her eyes shimmer with unshed tears as she falls to her knees at my feet. "He...he sacrificed himself. For me."

Galenia, the most nurturing of all of us, rushes over and throws her arms around her. Michaela buries her face in Galenia's shoulder and cries. I walk off to give her some privacy, and Horatia follows me.

"What just happened? What exactly did we witness, Penn? What on Earth was Webber doing here?" Horatia asks as we watch the house.

"I think it was the end of..." Of what? Our friend? That's playing it a bit fast and loose with the word *friend.*

"It was the end of Webber," I say, feeling sad for what's happened. As much as I didn't like him, he didn't deserve that. Now he's nothing. He's not at peace, but he's not being tortured either; he has just ceased to exist. It's the worst possible outcome for a heavenly soul.

"How?" she asks, grappling to understand what she's just seen. We all are.

"I don't know. Clearly, Mara is a formidable human."

"Formidable. Terrifying. Whatever," she says, not taking her eyes off the house.

"What was Webber doing here, Michaela?"

"He came to save me," she says in a shaky voice. "He found me in Mara's thread, told Ryker how to find me, and then Ryker brought him here. But he left him alone. I can't understand why he did that. If he'd stayed, maybe…" She trails off. She's staring in the direction we came, as if Webber might come through the woods at any moment.

"I'm sure Ryker knew what he was doing, Michaela. After all, Webber did save you. Isn't that what he came to do?" Galenia soothes.

"But his sacrifice seems so needless," she says before dissolving into silent sobs.

"Redemption comes in many forms, dear Reaper. You know that," Galenia says as she smoothes Michaela's hair.

Michaela's tears slow to a steady trickle, and we stand in silence for a few moments. Then Horatia poses another question. "Penn, what are we going to do?" It's barely above a whisper, and I know she needs an answer, not some joke to make her laugh or some philosophical BS. An actual answer. She needs direction.

"I think we should wait for nightfall."

Once Michaela's tears are all shed, for now at least, she and Galenia join us at the edge of the forest.

"Well, what do you think?" Michaela asks, her voice thick with grief.

I turn to her. She has twigs and leaves in her hair, her face is red, and her eyes are swollen. She's an absolute mess. While I didn't love the soul she's mourning, it breaks my heart to see her in such pain.

Taking her in my arms, I smooth her glossy hair and try to collect some of the leaves from it. "I'm sorry. I never meant for any of this to happen," I say, as if that will make anything better.

"I know," she says, and I feel her arms slowly wrap around me. I find myself enjoying her embrace. It feels like home.

"You saw what he did, right?" she asks.

"I did," I say. It was a beautiful gesture—so out of character for the Webber I've known for centuries. The way he purposefully drew Mara's attention away from Michaela, making as

84

much of a commotion as possible to tip Michaela off to the coming danger... And then throwing himself on her, taking the full force of Mara's attack. It's still hard to believe he did such a thing.

We don't speak again. We just stand there in the woods, holding each other, trying to make the world recognizable again with a single embrace. When it doesn't happen, we pull away, and she edges her way to the tree line, staring at the house.

Galenia joins her, offering silent comfort, and I settle in on her other side. Horatia holds vigil on the edge of our little gathering, watching for God knows what.

"I don't think Mara knows you survived her attack, Michaela," I say. "And she definitely doesn't know we're here. We have the upper hand. What do you know about the house?" I had only seen a small part of it while watching the threads. Any insight she can give us from actually having been inside will be helpful.

"I know it has a really dark basement," she says as she grips her arms across her chest.

"And?"

"It's a typical human house. Kitchen, couple of bedrooms, bathroom, living room, and an extensive library on witchcraft and the afterlife." She's irritated for some reason. "What do you want to know, Penn?"

"Who's inside?"

"Mara and her son Shiloh. This is all about him. She's using the threads to keep his soul here. It's horrible. He's trapped in that house indefinitely. He knows he doesn't belong, but there's not a thing he can do about it." Her voice wavers, and I can tell she's close to tears again.

"I know. What about Nathair?" I ask.

"He's here, and he's with her," she says with a nod. "But I didn't see him earlier. Did you? After what she did to Webber, everything went white. He usually isn't far away from her, so maybe she sent him on some errand. Or to collect another thread." She shudders.

"I heard her talking to him," I say, knowing he will present a complication.

"I know you're anxious to stop Mara now, but we came here for Michaela," Horatia says. "And here she is. Let's go. We're ill equipped for this mission. And we have other things to think about. Kismet and Andrew for one. We can come back later with reinforcements."

At the mention of their names, I cringe. We do need to save them...and soon. But if we don't stop Mara, none of that will matter.

"We can't leave Mara here to do what she wants," I say. "If we do, the cycle will just continue. The girl Michaela collected has certainly joined Kismet and Andrew in the prison of souls by now."

"Lily," Michaela breathes. "Yes, Mara and Nathair took her from me at the gates of heaven."

"This cycle won't stop until *we* stop it," I say. "We have to do something." I gesture toward the house to emphasize my point.

"But I don't think Michaela—"

She cuts Galenia off. "I'm fine. I know we need to get her. That's why Webber was out there in the first place. I wanted to figure out a way to stop Mara, and he wanted to leave. So I told him to wait outside for me. I sent him to slaughter."

"If he hadn't been out there, you would've been caught off guard by Mara's return. And you certainly wouldn't be here right now to discuss it with us. Stop guilt-tripping yourself—it's not helpful," I say. My tone's a little harsh, and I realize I'm angry about what Webber did. The whole thing just seems so...unnecessary. If they'd sent someone more capable to rescue Michaela, this never would've happened. He'd still be back home, waiting to jab us with some inappropriate comment. Instead, he's just gone. Forever.

Michaela looks at me, and I can tell she's trying to understand what I'm going through. It's something she always does when she's confused by someone's tone or actions. But judging by the look on her face, she doesn't come to any solid conclusions. Neither do I.

"My point remains," she says. "We can't just leave her here.

If we do, we'll have to come right back in a few days. By then, there will be more souls in the prison to rescue," she says.

"So," Horatia says from behind us. "This is where we transition from a rescue mission to seek and destroy." It's a statement, not a question.

"No. It's…recovery, I guess. We need to bring her back to the heavens in one piece. We are not equipped to deal with her. To judge her. And thank goodness for that," Michaela says. Her answer astounds me. Why *wouldn't* we judge her? We've all seen firsthand what this woman has done—the destruction she's wrought. If I had my way, we'd bring her straight to hell to let the demons take care of her punishment.

Michaela is watching me, and it's almost as if she reads my thoughts. "You wrote her Fate, Penn. It's not for us to decide to take that away from her."

A sigh escapes me, but only because I know she's right. "So now what?" I ask, feeling defeated.

"Now, we wait," she answers, although I have no idea what we will do when the time comes. This woman is capable of shriveling even the best-laid plans.

SIXTEEN

Michaela

As the sun sets, we head deeper into the woods to discuss our plan. Sitting in a circle, we each toss out what we think is the best way to capture Mara.

"We're safest if she's unconscious," I say, offering a jumping-off point. "We all saw what she did to Webber, and there's nothing to stop her from doing the same to all of us. We can't risk facing her when she's awake."

"Why don't we knock her over the head with a shovel or something? I think I saw one around back," Penn suggests, totally deadpan.

I can't tell if he's kidding or not. His expression is so serious. Horatia and Galenia don't laugh, and I just look at him. "Are you being serious?"

He shrugs. "Yeah. Why not? It'll knock her out." He's serious. He wants to use violence against her. Although I know she won't come quietly, I'm not sure bashing her over the head is the most elegant option. The image of four shovel-wielding heavenly beings almost makes me want to laugh. All we need is a light shining down on us from above—the humans love to depict us that way—to complete the picture. I stifle my snort and shake my head.

"It might kill her if you hit her too hard," I say, trying to point out why we might want to go for a safer approach.

"So. Let the demons deal with her."

"I have to say, death by shovel wasn't what I had in mind for her when I planned her death," Galenia offers. "She was supposed to die peacefully, albeit alone, but without suffering in her old age. I figured she'd suffered enough losses; she didn't need to suffer in death."

"See, she won't die when I hit her," Penn says.

"I don't think that's quite what Galenia meant," I say, getting exasperated.

Penn's tone turns quiet. "She's strayed a long way from what any of us had planned for her. Yes, we made her a grey thread, and they can go either way, but she wasn't totally black to start with. She did that on her own."

I feel out of place as the three Fates consider what their creation has done with the life they gave her. Suddenly, I hear Webber's voice in my mind.

Seeing the three of them working so flawlessly together... Well, it wasn't something I could ever be included in.

True, I feel left out, but I don't feel jealous. I feel sort of privileged to witness such magic.

I sigh, trying to shake Webber from my mind for the moment, and come back to the problem at hand. "Shiloh is very sick. There are a lot of medical supplies in the house." I turn to Galenia. "Do you think there's something we could use to knock her out?"

Galenia is well versed in how to kill the humans. It is, after all, her job. I can only hope she knows how to pull it back a little. Of course, neither of the sister Fates has expressed an opinion about what we should do with Mara. They've stayed noticeably quiet while Penn and I debate.

"I would have to see what's in there. But I can probably come up with something. I mean, even some cleaners will do it. Although they'll do some damage in the process." She cringes a little as she says it, shrugging apologetically. Nope. She's not a killer, at least not beyond the scope of her on-the-job duties. I sigh gratefully.

"We'll make do. So after we subdue her, we get the heck out of the house. Right?" I say, feeling good about the plan.

"And Nathair?" Horatia asks.

I slump. "I almost forgot about him."

"He's just a Reaper. He won't be nearly as much of a challenge as Mara. If we see him, we'll subdue him. Or chase him off. Either way, it's Mara we're after," Penn says.

"Just a Reaper, huh? Thanks a lot." The comment stings more than it should. Maybe I'm just overly emotional given everything that's happened.

"I didn't mean it like that." His voice is soft, and he reaches across the circle to pat my knee.

I move back. "Yes, you did. You meant it exactly like that. You think he'll be easy to overcome because he's just a Reaper. We're all nothing compared to you. Is that right?" What's wrong with me? I'm so angry all of a sudden, but really, I don't think I'm mad at Penn. He's a victim here, just like the rest of us are. I'm angry at the situation, at the world, at Mara, but definitely not at Penn. I feel a little like I did when we were wandering through hell. Full of irrational anger and disappointment. Infected by the dark feelings around me.

"No. What is happening right now?" He looks from Galenia to Horatia, but they're both giving him accusatory looks. Horatia even has one eyebrow raised at him. At least they're on my side.

"Michaela, I'm sorry. I didn't mean to hurt you. I only meant that he isn't as powerful as Mara. Dealing with him will be comparatively easy. He's one of us. We know what to expect from him." He scoots closer to me, putting both hands on my shoulders. I look away. "You're the one who's got us this far, Michaela. We wouldn't have even known about the prison of souls if not for you, and we certainly wouldn't have been able to save anyone from hell on our own. We wouldn't even know where to find Mara if not for you. And we definitely wouldn't be this close to stopping her."

He takes hold of my chin and turns my face toward him.

"You know we need you," he continues in a softer voice. "*I* need you. We came here for you. Don't forget that."

I know he's telling the truth. Webber's initial motivation was to save himself. Penn came here for me.

"We can't be at each other's throats like this. Not if we're going to save the world. You can bicker with me all you want after that job is done, okay?" He smiles down at me, and I can't help but smile back.

"No. I don't like bickering with you. It makes me feel terrible."

"Okay, so we won't fight. Whatever you want. Let's just get the heck out of here first. Then we can plan the rest of our existence." The way he says it catches me. As if he plans to spend the rest of eternity *with* me. But of course, he didn't mean just me. He meant all of us. We're friends, and friends stick together. Still, the way he's looking deep into my eyes...well, it feels more personal. And I can't deny the happiness that thought gives me.

Once darkness has fallen in earnest and all the lights are out, we sneak up to the house, trying not to draw attention to ourselves. We've decided to go in through the front. The bedrooms are both smack dab in the middle of the house, separated by the bathroom, but Mara's bedroom is closer to the back door. We slink up the front steps, and I swear they creek deliberately, as if announcing our intrusion.

The front door isn't even locked. Really, who would she need to keep out now that she thinks Webber and I are toast? It's who she's trying to keep *in* that matters.

The four of us ease our way into the dark house, and Penn closes the door behind us.

"Now what?" he whispers.

Pointing toward the bathroom, I take Galenia's hand. Then I gesture to Horatia and Penn to keep a look out—pointing to my eyes, and then the windows. It makes me feel foolish, like I'm part of some intense espionage movie, but they get the idea. Horatia takes a position near the front door, and Penn follows us to the edge of the hallway to stand watch there.

Silently, Galenia and I pad into the bathroom. Speaking in barely a whisper, I tell her, "Shiloh's room is right next door. We need to be as quiet as possible. We don't need to worry him anymore. He's been through enough as it is."

Nodding gravely, she gets to work. She doesn't even need to open the medicine cabinet. There are jars and bottles of things everywhere, just like I remember. I watch as Galenia mixes a few liquid chemicals together in an empty bottle she finds under the sink. I have no idea what she's doing, but her work is quiet and efficient.

When she's finished, she looks around the bathroom for a moment, and then grabs a hand towel. The ring that's holding it clangs against the wall, and we both tense. Penn is at the door in an instant, standing with his back to us in a protective stance. I can't see Horatia, but I'm sure she's nearby. No one in the house stirs, thank goodness.

It feels like we're hiding from the demons in hell again. Maybe we are. This woman is like no human I've ever encountered. I know what made her this way, but I still can't understand why she chose this path, let alone why she continues to choose it. She's been to hell, so how can she ignore the inevitable consequences of her actions? But I suppose that's the problem. She thinks she's too powerful for consequences. It will be a dark day when she realizes that no one can avoid the end of the road they've chosen to walk.

Once we're sure it's safe, Galenia dumps some of the liquid onto the towel. We leave the bathroom, and I lead the way to Mara's bedroom, Penn and Galenia falling in beside me. Horatia is right behind us. With agonizing steadiness, he eases the door open. It doesn't make a sound at all.

Her room is darker than the hallway, and a sliver of light pours in with every inch we open the door further. Horatia waits outside to keep watch for Nathair or anything else that might disturb our sleeping quarry.

Galenia moves forward wordlessly, and we all hold our breath as she suspends the cloth just above Mara's mouth. Penn moves to the other side of her bed, ready to grab her if she fights. But it's not necessary. Galenia is so soft, slow, and gentle that Mara barely stirs as the cloth is lowered over her face.

Soon, her breathing becomes unnaturally deep, and we know it worked. Galenia did it. All we have to do is grab her and go. But something keeps us there, staring at this human who has caused us so much pain.

"We should kill her right now," Penn suggests, his voice dark. "She's helpless. We could end this here and now. Let another Reaper take her to hell," Penn suggests.

I'd be lying if I said it wasn't tempting, but I can't do it.

"You are like a dog with a bone," I say quietly, not wanting to disturb Shiloh.

Surprisingly, Horatia comes to my rescue. "Michaela is right, Penn. We aren't killers. Could you really snuff out her life if it came down to it? Right here? Right now?"

He hesitates and looks down at the human. The moonlight is shining through the edge of her curtain in a small sliver that lands right next to her face, casting an eerie glow on her. "Yes," he finally says. "I believe I could. She's strayed far enough from her Fate."

"You are thinking of Andrew. And Kismet. And all the other ways she wronged you," I say, putting my hand on his shoulder.

"Two wrongs don't make a right?" he says. "Maybe not. But she's committed far more than one wrong…"

"Either way, we're ending it. And I would much prefer for her blood to be on someone else's hands," I say, bringing my other hand up to his shoulder, trying to pull him back toward me, toward the light.

He doesn't budge. My breath catches in my throat when he bends down over Mara. But instead of strangling her or snuffing out her life in some way, he hoists her up and lifts her over his shoulder.

"Good God, she's a lot heavier than those souls we took out of hell," he says. I stifle a giggle. Souls weigh almost nothing, and this human's unfamiliar weight is clearly posing a challenge to Penn.

"Come on," I say. "You're a big, strong man. Surely, you can carry one tiny woman."

He bumps into me accidently on purpose as he walks past me with Mara hanging limply over his back. "Oh. Excuse me," he says as he walks out of her bedroom.

Galenia keeps a tight hold on the cloth drenched with her concoction as she follows him. Horatia goes next, leaving me alone in the room of the woman who has done the world more harm than any human I've ever seen in my centuries as a Reaper.

Have we really just ended it? Is it over? I know we still have to collect the other souls who are caught in the prison, but now that we have Mara, even that should be easier. The hard part is over, right?

But as I stand there alone in the dark, something tells me it's too good to be true.

SEVENTEEN

Penn

I'm already hustling out the front door when I notice no one is following me. Lugging this dead-weight human over my shoulder isn't exactly easy, and I know it's a long walk back to the mists. I'd like to get going. Who knows how long she'll be out? We can't afford to dillydally.

I adjust Mara on my shoulder and turn around. The girls are standing in the back of the living room, peering down the hall. Michaela is standing next to the door to the other bedroom—Shiloh's room.

I sigh. "Michaela," I whisper. "We don't have time for this."

She closes the gap between us so rapidly I take a reflexive step back.

"There is *always* time to do the right thing."

"And in this case, the right thing is…" I trail off, hoping she'll fill in the gap.

"I want to tell Shiloh what's happened. He deserves to know that he'll be at peace soon."

"Nathair could be anywhere. We will send someone back for the boy, but we can't risk wasting more time. I'm going to vote for exiting as quickly as possible. Anyone else?" I look to

Galenia and Horatia for help with this one.

Galenia puts an arm on Michaela's shoulder. "I think we should go." She says it quietly, as if the soft words will be easier for Michaela to hear.

"Me too," Horatia adds. "Nathair is too much of a question mark. We need to go while the getting's good."

Michaela's face falls, and I can see the struggle play out on her face. She knows the truth, but her heart doesn't want any part of it. She wants to be with the little boy in his time of need. It's one of the things I love about her, but right now, it's not working in our favor.

"He'll be okay, Michaela. Someone will be here to pick him up before he realizes what's happened," I say, trying to soothe her with a best-case scenario.

"I don't know about that. But his suffering is almost at an end, whether he knows it or not. I guess that will have to be enough for now."

We head out into the night, and I scan the area uneasily.

"He could be anywhere," Horatia whispers.

"Let's hope he isn't anywhere we need to be."

Michaela is silent as she looks around.

We pad quietly across the lawn, making it to the edge of the woods without incident. I want to stop and rest, but I wouldn't let Michaela stop to talk to the boy, so I can hardly justify it. We still have a long way to go.

Something triggers an alert in my mind as we walk. A sound that makes the hairs on my arm stand on end.

"Did you guys hear that?" I say, barely above a whisper.

The others stop in their tracks, and we all look around. Mara starts to stir, and Galenia is on her like lightning. But the moan she made was loud in the quiet wood. If someone's out there, they know we are too.

Once Mara is out again, we stand with our backs together, creating a perimeter, searching all sides of the woods around us for the source of the original sound. But we come up empty.

"He's out there," Michaela says.

"Who?" Galenia asks.

"Nathair."

Galenia's breath catches. "How do you know?"

"I can feel him, a fellow Reaper. It's him."

We stand in silence, waiting for him to make a move. When he doesn't, none of us really knows what to do. I certainly don't want to stand here for hours with an unconscious human on my back. But part of me fears we may be walking right into a trap if we continue making our way toward the mists.

"What should we do?" Galenia finally whispers.

"We should keep going. I think he's just following us for now," Michaela says. "Be on your guard."

As if we weren't already.

Finally, after what felt like hours, we arrive at the dome. Michaela is stunned by it, and it is quite a sight. The mists billow up against the invisible wall, creating a foggy ceiling above our heads.

"So this is what it looks like," she breathes as she stares up at it in wonder.

"Yup," I say, shifting Mara on my shoulder. "Not to keep you from ogling this curiosity or anything, but we better get going."

Horatia, Galenia, and I step through the dome, but Michaela doesn't follow. She's probably still looking at the mists.

"Now what?" I ask, trying and failing to hide my impatience.

"I'll just go check on her," Horatia says as she walks back through the wall.

But she doesn't reemerge. I start counting my heartbeats, and when I get to one hundred, I take a step toward the dome. Galenia's face is wrought with worry as I lay Mara down, leaning her against a tree.

"You stay here with her. Keep her out. I'll be right back," I assure her. I can only hope it's true.

I'm not sure what I'll find on the other side of the wall, but

I have a feeling Michaela and Horatia aren't just enjoying the view anymore.

I've never been so disappointed to be right.

A man dressed in the black-and-white garb of a Reaper has Michaela in a chokehold. His free hand covers her mouth. Horatia is standing in front of him, her hands outstretched, as if she's trying to negotiate with him.

"What's going on here?" I say, impatient and exhausted. "Seriously, Nathair. What are you thinking right now? Why would you take one of your own as a hostage? Besides, there are still three of us and one of you. You can't win this."

"You'd think so, wouldn't you?" he says, his voice lower and more sinister than I expected. I wonder if it always sounded that way, or if his time on Earth—with Mara—has changed him.

Michaela thrashes a little in his arms, and he leans in and whispers in her ear. She screams beneath his hand, but he holds her fast.

I take a slow step forward, and he matches me by taking a step back, dragging Michaela with him.

"What's your master plan here, Nathair? What exactly do you want at this point?" I say.

"Even trade. Mara for Michaela. No one needs to get hurt. I'll just take her back to the house, and you guys can continue on your way. She'll be none the wiser," Nathair says.

"*No*," Michaela shouts through his hand. It's muffled, but I can tell what she wants.

"I'm afraid I'm not going to do that, Nathair. We're taking Mara back. If we leave her here, more people *will* get hurt. Whatever you had going on with her is done," I say.

I can tell it's not what he expected by the uneasy way he shifts his weight from side to side. He honestly thought I'd trade and that would be the end of it. While it would be absolute torture to leave Michaela behind, it's obvious this isn't an offer she wants me to accept. No, if it comes to that, I'll have to leave and come back for her. But I hope it won't come to that.

Sure enough, my Reaper rescues herself. Michaela seizes the other Reaper's moment of unease and bites his hand. He cries out in pain and loosens his grip on her, giving her the opportunity to stomp on his foot. She tries to run from him. Grabbing a handful of her hair, he yanks her back. Screaming in pain, she falls backward to the ground.

Horatia steps in and tries to free her, pounding on him, and I rush to their aid. The Reaper's so busy dealing with Horatia's fists, he doesn't see me coming around behind him. It's all too easy to get his hands behind his back and restrain him.

Michaela scrambles away, tears streaming down her face as she looks back at him. She's not just physically hurt; she's been attacked by someone she should have been able trust—an old coworker.

"What should we do with him?" Horatia asks.

My mind is racing. What *can* we do with him? I can't restrain him *and* carry Mara. And I know the girls can't handle him, not all the way back at least. They might be able to carry Mara if they work together, but if she starts to wake up, one of them will need to sedate her.

Michaela is the one who offers a solution. Her voice is low and dark, and it gives me chills. "I think we should lock him in the basement."

"I…what?" I say.

"It's no worse than what he did to me. Someone can come back for him after we've told everyone in the heavens what he's done," she says. She's dead serious. She wants me to walk all the way back to the house with this lunatic and lock him in the basement.

"But that will take forever." It comes out as a bit of a whine, but my point remains valid.

"Well, what do you suggest, Penn? What if he escapes us in the mists? Overwhelms us while we're trying to manage Mara? He could ruin everything. I'm not sure that's a risk I want to take," Horatia says. Once again, I'm caught off guard by one of my sisters siding with someone else. Normally, we're all so in sync.

"Can we even keep Mara out for that long? It's going to take a few hours. And I think one of you should come with me. If he gets squirrely, it'll be easier for two of us to restrain him." Wait, did I just agree with them? I shake my head in frustration. "For the record, I still don't think this is a good idea."

"I'll go ask Galenia what she thinks. She can be the tie-breaker, okay?"

"Fine," I say. Nathair's struggling in my arms, making me less than excited about what lies ahead. "Hurry up, will you? This isn't my favorite thing." He thrashes around and tries to head butt me, as if to emphasize my point.

Horatia nods and hurries back through the wall of mists. She's back faster than I thought she would be.

"The two of us will go with you. Galenia says she's fine on her own. We'll run back here when we're done to make up the time, okay?"

"Run?" The thought only exhausts me further. "I'm not sure I'll have the energy for that."

"You better find it, because you'll have to carry Mara back through the mists when we're done," Horatia says. She's not trying to make me feel worse; she's just stating the facts. Still, the facts feel almost as heavy as Nathair.

"You couldn't have just left us alone?" The bitterness I feel toward the man I'm restraining comes through in my voice.

He responds by trying to head butt me again. I dodge him easily and sigh. "It's going to be like that the whole way back, isn't it?" I turn to Horatia. "Think Galenia's concoction will work on this one?"

She snorts. "I don't think Galenia is sharing, particularly not for heavenly beings. Besides, it probably won't have the same effect on him."

I nod. "No probably not." He tries the head-butt maneuver again, and I curse under my breath.

"I'm not going down without a fight," Nathair insists.

I can't help but roll my eyes. "Hate to break it to you, Captain Obvious, but you already went down with the ship."

About halfway back to the house, the fight goes out of Nathair.

He starts walking along with me, as if he's accepted his fate, but I don't loosen my grip on him. For all I know, he's trying to lull me into a false sense of security. He's a loose cannon who's in league with a woman who's earned herself a one-way ticket to hell. My trust went out the door as soon as I found out he was a willing accomplice.

"So, Nathair, tell me. How did you meet Mara?" I ask. Part of me just wants to break the silence and monotony of our walk, but another part genuinely wants to know how a Reaper could turn so far from his intended path. Okay, so maybe that's the pot calling the kettle black—I am a banished Fate, after all—but I still want to know.

He doesn't respond for so long, I don't think he ever will.

Michaela's the one who gets him talk. "How did you stray so far from your roots?" she asks softly.

His face twists into a condescending sneer as he looks at Michaela. I want to slap him, but my hands are otherwise occupied. I already regret trying to engage him in conversation.

"My roots? My roots didn't go very deep."

"Clearly," Michaela says.

"No one appreciated me, least of all that asshole Ryker. He's too holier-than-thou for my taste, even for a heavenly being. When Mara showed up at one of my assignments and told me she needed a hand, I was more than willing to help her out."

Michaela was quiet for a few paces, and I could tell she was reflecting on his words.

"You love her, don't you?"

I stop dead, making Nathair jerk a little. Honestly, I don't know what I expected her to say. But romance wasn't high on the list.

"*Hey*," he shouts.

"Sorry," I say, even though I'm not.

He doesn't answer her question, but now I'm intrigued. If she's right, it would certainly explain what he's done. I surprised myself by the lengths I was willing to go to for love. I think about Kismet withering away in the prison of souls and push Nathair a little harder.

"You do love her, don't you?" I say.

He doesn't need to answer me now. His silence is confirmation enough.

"What did she offer you, Nathair?" Michaela asks. "Did she say she loved you back? Were you dumb enough to believe her? The only one she truly loves is Shiloh. You know that, right?"

I'm shocked by her response. I've never heard something so harsh come out of Michaela's mouth, even if it *is* the truth. She's madder than I've ever seen her.

"Shut up," Nathair barks. "Of course she loves me. Once Shiloh's safe, we're going to go somewhere where no one will ever find us. We're going to be a family." As soon as the words are out, I can tell he regrets revealing his vulnerability to us. He turns away from her and walks faster, jerking me behind him for a change, as if he wants to get away from Michaela.

"Shiloh is the only man in her life," I say, "and he's the only one there will ever be. She's a Spinner in her own right—weaving lies, trapping innocents in her web." I cluck a few times, as if what's happened to him is a shame. "Do you think they'll take pity on you for your soft heart?"

He tries to head butt me again. I start to laugh, and then something occurs to me. I saw him question her. His unease at her methods. "You're not so tough are you, Nathair? You don't like what she's doing, at least not all of it. I heard you trying to get her to stop putting them in the prison. You know what she's doing is wrong. Why abandon that completely?"

His voice is a little sad. "Like you said, I boarded the ship. There wasn't any turning back. Might as well go down with it."

I have no response. He's so matter-of-fact. The situation is so ridiculous I can't get my mind around it. A Spinner in love with his own creation. A Reaper in love with a human witch. How in the world did we get so off course?

By the time we get there, it's almost sunrise.

"We need to work fast, or we'll wake up Shiloh," Michaela says. "If he's not already awake.

"What can Shiloh do to us?" I ask, legitimately not understanding what danger he could pose.

"Nothing more than a delay. If he sees us, we'll have some explaining to do. I'm worried about leaving Galenia alone with that woman for so long. We need to get back to her."

Horatia speaks for the first time since we left our sister behind. "She's stronger than she looks. Honestly, I'm not a bit worried about her."

Part of me is surprised by her response, but I realize she's right. Galenia looks slight, but she isn't. She has a calming power that can overcome even the angriest adversary. She will be fine. Besides, I have no doubt that her concoction will keep Mara from doing any harm.

We ease our way into the house and pad down the hall. Michaela hesitates in front of Shiloh's door, but I shake my head. She nods as she leads the way to the basement.

It's harder to restrain Nathair as we go down the stairs, and he struggles enough to create a commotion. If Shiloh didn't already know we were here, he does now. Maybe he'll assume Nathair is just roughing Webber and Michaela around. It's a dark thought, but I hope it's enough to keep him in his room.

We eventually get the rogue Reaper to the bottom, and Michaela leads us into a small, dark room.

"What *is* this place?" I ask.

"It's Mara's prison on Earth. It's where she kept me...and then Webber and me," Michaela answers.

"Should we tie him up?" Horatia asks.

"Tie him to the pole. That's what they did to me," Michaela says coldly. "Let's see him get out of that."

Horatia grabs some rope off the wall, and I force Nathair to sit down in front of the pole in the center of the room.

"Who puts a giant pole in the middle of a small room like this? I mean, it really renders the room useless," I say as I restrain Nathair's thrashing. He's fighting us right up to the end.

"I'm sure Mara will be grateful for your decorating advice," Horatia says as she binds Nathair's hands.

The three of us turn to look at him before we leave the

room. "Well, goodbye for now. Someone will be back shortly to collect you," Michaela says.

He spits at us, but it doesn't have enough force behind it to even reach our feet.

"Yup. I think that about sums up how we feel about you," I say.

We turn to leave, but a little boy is standing at the bottom of the stairs, blocking our way. Shiloh.

"What are you doing here?" he demands.

"Shiloh. You shouldn't be up. Go back to bed," Michaela insists.

"I told you to leave hours ago. What's going on? Who are they?" He fires the questions off one after another. They almost bowl me over, but Michaela seems to instantly know what to do. She goes to him—stopping just short of touching him—and ushers him back up the stairs. She's murmuring softly to him, but I can't hear what she's saying. Turning, I take one last look at Nathair tied to the post before I shut the door and lock it. I kind of think he would've flipped me off if his hands weren't tied behind his back. His eyes are full of the kind of hatred humans usually reserve for each other. It feels out of place in a heavenly being.

As I slide the lock home, I find myself wishing we had a chair or something else to put in front of it. I mean, Michaela escaped from here, twice. What's to say he won't do the same? I sigh. All we need to do is buy ourselves enough time to get back to the mists. If he escapes, someone else will find him. Without Mara, he's mostly powerless.

Horatia leads the way up the stairs, into the empty hallway. The door to Shiloh's room is open, and I can see her sitting on the boy's bed. She's still talking to him in that same soothing voice.

He's so gaunt it's almost painful to look at him. His brown hair is dull in the dim light of the bedroom, and he's so thin I can see his collarbone under his t-shirt. He's literally wasting away. What parent would want this existence for her child? I know Michaela said we aren't equipped to judge Mara, but I can't help myself. The anger makes me restless.

I stalk into the living room and start to pace a large circle around the space. Horatia joins me.

"What's wrong?" she asks quietly as she leans against the doorway leading to the hall.

I keep my voice low to avoid drawing the boy's attention. "Look what she's done to that poor boy! She doesn't deserve a fair trial."

"You'd better calm down before Michaela finds you like this," she says, offering no words of comfort, agreement, or disagreement. It's Horatia's blunt way.

I know she's right. I need to cool it, but I can't. Seeing this little boy's suffering has pushed me over the edge. I know it's affecting Horatia too. After all, she's the one who cut his thread short. And to see it made unnaturally long…

I can see the pain I'm feeling mirrored on her face.

"Do you think we could've changed things, Ratia? Used more care when we made her and the boy? Done things differently?"

She crosses the room and falls into my open arms. It's the only answer I need. She feels the same pain I do over our wayward creation. We stand that way, trying to give each other strength, until Michaela joins us.

"Let's go," she says as she walks past us, clearly eager to get out of the house.

"Hey," Horatia calls out, but Michaela doesn't stop. Horatia breaks away from me and goes after her, with me right on her heels.

"Hey," she calls out again.

Michaela keeps right on walking. "Let's *go*," she shouts, not even turning her head to look at us. She just charges forward toward the woods.

Horatia breaks into a run and catches up, grabbing her arm.

"Hey," she says, turning Michaela to face her. We're about halfway to the woods, standing in the middle of the yard. I'm a little uncomfortable to stand here so exposed, but I know better than to say anything.

"Hey yourself," Michaela says. "We need to get back to Galenia."

"Are you okay?" Horatia asks.

"No. I'm not," Michaela chokes out. "I just had to tell a boy that his mother is being taken before God to answer for her crimes. He's not grieving his mother's death, he's mourning her eternal soul, if there's even anything left of it when God is done with her."

Horatia takes her shaking hand, trying to steady her.

"But it doesn't matter if I'm okay. I'm not important in this. Mara is important. Shiloh is important." She looks at me. "Kismet, Andrew, and Lily are important. We have to get back."

I nod. But while she's right, while I know we should already be running toward the mists with every last bit of energy we possess, I hug her instead. And then I sweep Horatia into the embrace as well.

"It will be okay," I say, drowning in a mass of blonde and brown hair and resisting the urge to blow it out of my face.

"And if it's not, we'll fight until it's over," Michaela finishes for me. I squeeze the two of them even harder, and we run back into the woods together.

When we find Galenia, morning is well on its way. She's sitting next to Mara, who's still completely out. She greets us with a warm smile when we come through the wall of mists.

"How did it go?" she asks as she stands up and brushes leaves and debris off her gold robe.

"I mean, it could've been worse," I say, shrugging, trying to hide the fact that I'm pretty out of breath.

"Shiloh saw us," Michaela says between pants, somehow knowing Galenia will understand the ramifications of that.

And she does. She gives her a huge, meaningful hug, as if trying to take all of our friend's sorrow in one single embrace.

"I'm sorry," I hear her whisper to Michaela.

"Me too," she says in return.

"Are we ready? How's she doing?" I nod toward Mara.

"She stirred twice. I'm concerned about what the chemicals might be doing to her. But we had no choice. When we get there, it becomes someone else's problem, right?" she says, clearly hoping we'll confirm her assumption.

Without hesitation, I answer, "Right."

Though I have no idea where the energy comes from—besides necessity—I manage to sling Mara back over my shoulder and start walking.

When I glance back, I see Michaela walking between my sisters, holding their hands.

"It feels good to be going home," she says as we walk deeper and deeper into the mists together.

I couldn't agree more.

EIGHTEEN

Michaela

The mists are soothing to my frayed nerves. I breathe them in as we walk, taking comfort from them, from the women at my sides. We've done it. We've ended it.

The urge to sit down and let the mists swallow me is overwhelming, but my companions keep my feet moving. I shut my eyes and breathe deeply.

When we get to the golden gate, we stand there—directionless. Not one of us wants to go through. It seems wrong to take such an evil being into our home. But we can't take her into hell either. They'll never let her go once they have her, however justified they may be. And while I doubt she'll be going to heaven, I think we all deserve to see her go to trial. Those of us who have been affected by Mara's chaos need closure. We need an explanation for what she's done.

Even so, I just can't bear to let this happen. "We can't bring her in there," I blurt out.

The Fates all stop in their tracks.

"Well, what do you want to do? I'm all for knocking on the black gate," Penn says, still hanging on to the hope that we can dump her on the demons and be done with it.

"Can you three wait out here with her? I'll go get some help." I'm adding yet another complication to our plan—and I know it—but I can't stomach the idea of bringing her in with us.

I look at the three Fates in front of me, waiting for them to respond. Penn sighs and sets her down in front of him. There's nothing for him to lean her against, so she just lies among the clouds. They're thick enough that they almost swallow her, making her look a little otherworldly. I frown down at her. I don't want to think of her as being at peace when the souls she trapped in hell are still stuck there.

"All right," I say. "I'll be right back."

Taking a deep breath, I push the golden gate open and go home.

No one is milling around on the other side, so I walk to Ryker's office unobstructed. It's morning here, so I know most of the Reapers are already out on assignment and won't stop me as I make my way through my home. I pick up the pace, saying a silent prayer that Ryker is actually in his office.

Hesitantly, I knock on the door. When no one answers, I knock a little louder. Just as I'm about to give up, the door swings open and Ryker takes me into his big arms, lifts me up, and spins me around. Just as quickly as he's done it, I'm back on the ground, facing him. He's standing straight as a board and looking down at me, as if the display of emotion never happened at all.

"Where have you been?" he demands.

I take a seat opposite his desk and tell him about Mara—her powers, what she did with them, and her apparent lack of remorse. Frowning, he turns to face a holographic image to his left.

I didn't see him touch anything, but suddenly, the image of one of hell's Guardians appears before me. I'm taken aback that he can communicate with them this way.

"I have a special assignment for you. There is an actual human outside your gate. Not a soul. I need you to...care for her until her appointed trial. No harm should come to her, but know that she is very powerful. Learned in our ways, and in the ways of witchcraft. She has eliminated two Archangels and a Spinner. Be forewarned."

The Guardian gives a big, toothy grin. Even though he's not really in the room with me, I want to shrink away. The smell of hell surrounds me—a memory so real, my pulse quickens. I shake myself and take a deep breath.

"It would be my pleasure," the Guardian growls out. "When is the trial?"

"Undetermined. When I know, you'll know."

The Guardian nods and his image disappears.

"Do you trust him?" I ask.

"No. You can never trust a demon. But I trust her less than I trust the demon. She needs to be restrained. I know the Guardian will be able to handle her." He leans back in his chair and smiles at me. "It's good to have you back. Now, tell me everything."

And I do. I start with Shiloh, Mara's motivation for what she did. When I get to the part about Nathair joining forces with her, I remember that he's still trapped in the basement.

Ryker pauses my soliloquy to dispatch a team to retrieve the wayward Reaper, and then asks me to continue.

When I get to the part about Webber, I'm suddenly furious with him. "Ryker, why did you leave him?"

"Do you want the long or the short answer?" he asks seriously.

"Both."

"Fine. I had obligations here. I couldn't stay with him."

The comment stings. "Obligations more important than me?"

His face softens. "I couldn't take your other friends to Earth, but I needed to make sure Miette was in the right place at the right time to help them find you."

It stops me dead.

"So what's the long answer?"

"Webber was distraught. He felt it was something he needed

to do on his own to earn his redemption. I wouldn't deny him that."

"That I can believe," I say, hoping my friend would be happy to know his sacrifice had not been wasted.

I keep talking until I've told Ryker the entire story. Eventually, I get to the part about the three souls still trapped in the prison of souls—Andrew, Kismet, and Lily—and their need to be rescued.

"I knew something extreme happened to put you in the healing ward with all those burns, but I had no idea it was something of this magnitude." Ryker slouches in his chair a little, seemingly weighed down by what I've said.

"But now that we have her, we can release them, right?" I say, hopeful it will be a non-issue.

"Of course. I will send Reapers to collect them immediately." He reaches for the holograph to summon someone, but I stop him.

"I'd like to get them, please. I started this. I'd like to finish it." I think about God's plan for me, for all of us. "I believe I'm meant to do it."

"I have another task for you, Michaela."

His words take the wind out of my sails. Another task? What could be more important than getting Andrew, Kismet, and Lily out of that terrible prison?

"I will send emissaries to hell to prepare the way for you. They'll make sure you don't face any…" He hesitates. "Obstacles. You can retrieve the souls when you're done with your mission."

I like the sound of that. An easy trip into hell? Yes, please. Penn and I barely made it out the last time.

"What's the mission?" A wave of wariness washes over me as I wait for his response.

"Another surprise has popped up." My heart sinks, but something about his expression tells me I've got it wrong. There's a sparkle in his eye. Still, my panic fights for attention. Another surprise? How can that be? We have Mara.

"Do you think Nathair escaped and is continuing her work?"

"No. I do not," he says simply.

"Well, then who?" I demand, dying to know the reason for his sly smile.

"It's a surprise, yes, but this person's name didn't show up on our list early. He should've been reaped years ago."

The name falls from my lips of its own accord. "Shiloh."

NINETEEN

Penn

The wait outside the gates is torturous. We are all silent. Galenia and Horatia sit near Mara, and I pace around near the edge of the mists. I'm not sure what to do with myself. I don't want to leave this human out in the middle of the three gates, where she might do even more damage, but I also don't want to be anywhere near her. She's destroyed everything that was important to me. Kismet and Andrew are lost to me forever. And then there are all those other threads she cut short. Frederico. Jeff. Pearl. Chesney. Nysa. Lily. That's not even to mention the thousands of ghosts created by her negligence. The lives ruined...

I take a deep breath to calm myself and keep pacing, hoping someone will come soon. Every few paces, I glance at the gold door, hoping someone will come through. But, to my dismay, the black gate comes into view. A demon steps out of it.

I've actually never seen a Guardian before, but I assume this is one of them. He certainly doesn't look human like the Warden we saw in hell, but he's bigger and more intimidating than the lesser demons we encountered there. The flames of hell show through the cracks in his charred skin. His fingers have long, black claws on them, and his arms are so long, he drags them through the clouds as he walks. His face is angular, almost like it was chiseled out of black stone. I make an effort not to shrink back from him. He's here for Mara, I'm sure.

Then another Guardian follows him out of the black gate. I look from them to my sisters, not exactly sure of what to do.

Galenia surprises me by standing up and approaching them. "Hello." Her voice is soft and soothing, but I'm not sure if it's meant to soothe them or us. Probably us, since they don't seem frightened at all.

"Fates," they acknowledge. Their whispery voices send a chill down my spine. "We hear you have something special for us."

"I'm not sure I'm comfortable leaving her with you. How do I know you'll bring her to the trial when she's needed?" Galenia asks, stepping between Mara and the Guardians.

"Our orders come from the head Reaper. We know this one comes with strings attached."

She turns to me. "Ryker."

I nod, and she steps aside.

A grotesque smile spreads across the larger Guardian's face as he looks down at her. "Tell us about this human," he says. "She doesn't seem so special to me."

"She took out two Archangels. Don't underestimate her," Horatia warns.

"Impressive." The larger Guardian continues to smile down at Mara, who's starting to stir.

Galenia goes to her, searching for the cloth, but the Guardian holds up his hand. "Maybe we should let her see what she's in for."

"I don't think that's a good idea," I say, backing away from Mara. I sincerely don't want to be around when she wakes up. She's going to be madder than a hornet when she figures out what we did, but the prospect of her rage seems to *excite* them. As if they feed on it. They probably do, now that I think about it.

Galenia backs away too, but Horatia goes toward the Guardians of all things. As soon as we realize what she's doing, we rush to join her.

"Hiding behind the demons, eh, Fates?" the smaller Guardian says with a chuckle.

"I'm not ashamed to acknowledge that you're better equipped to deal with this situation," Galenia says.

The smaller one looks back at her for a moment, as if he isn't quite sure what to make of her, and then returns his gaze to his quarry.

"It's nice to meet you, Mara," the larger Guardian says.

She's sitting up slowly, moaning. "What the hell did you do to me?" Her voice is hoarse, and she's coughing. Leaning forward, she puts her head between her knees and vomits into the clouds.

"She really is human," the smaller Guardian notes.

"That she is," I confirm.

"This will be interesting," he says.

Wiping her mouth with the back of her hand, she staggers to standing. "Who are you?" she demands. It's obvious she's not even a little afraid of these creatures from hell.

The moment her eyes lock on to us, she scoffs and says, "More Fates. How many of you do I have to kill to get you to leave me alone? You're nothing but a nuisance!" She raises her hands, and we shrink down behind the Guardians.

The demons laugh. They actually laugh, and the sound is horrible. It's like cold wind hissing through the slats in a dark, drafty barn. It surrounds us, and I feel like we'll never be warm and happy again.

Mara starts to mutter something, calling upon her powers, but the Guardians are laughing so hard it whips up a wind. Or maybe Mara is the one who's creating the wind. The girls' hair whips wildly around their faces as the demons' terrifying laughter rises in volume.

Mara stays focused on us, but the Guardians' amusement finally dies when sparks appear on her fingertips.

"Enough," the larger Guardian says, and her hands go jerkily to her sides. The sparks disappear, but her eyes glow with anger.

"Hey," I whisper, sensing she's not nearly done. They ignore me.

"Dispergeretur." I can actually see the word leave her mouth and curl through the air, floating toward the smaller Guardian, the one Galenia is hiding behind. The larger Guardian doesn't seem to see it, but the smaller one watches with amused fascination as the word curls around him. It reaches his leg before working its way up his body, around his arm, over his head, around his other arm, and back down his other leg. His smirk finally fades by the time he's covered in silvery light.

Mara is smiling as she watches it happen, her arms still stiff at her sides. The Guardian must be holding her.

All of a sudden, the light suddenly caves in on itself, leaving nothing behind. The Guardian standing in front of Galenia vanishes in thin air, leaving Galenia exposed.

Before the human can do any more damage, the lone Guardian roars with anger. I feel the vibration of it in my chest. Galenia runs over to us, and we three Fates wrap our arms around each other and shamelessly cower behind the demon.

The Guardian closes the distance between himself and Mara faster than I've ever seen any being move. He clogs her over the head with a closed fist, and she goes down with a thump.

"There are some benefits to working with humans instead of souls," he says, looking down at her body.

He picks her up like she weighs no more than a feather, and her head lolls a little. I cringe when I see it.

"What's the matter, Fate? Not comfortable with a little violence?" He jostles her around a little more, and her head rolls around limply. It's odd. I'm worried she might be dead. Why does *that* bother me? I wanted the demons to take her. To kill her. But I'm starting to realize Michaela was right—we aren't made for killing. I want Mara to get that trial Michaela thinks she deserves.

The Guardian laughs at me, as if reading my thoughts. "I didn't kill her. But she'll be out for a bit, the damned fool." He says nothing of his fallen comrade. I don't even know if demons form relationships with one another. It wouldn't really be hell if good things existed there.

"Well, it's been fun, Fates," he says as he carries her back toward the black gate. "I'm sure I'll be seeing you soon."

"Wait," Galenia calls after him. She runs over to a low-lying cloud and grabs the bottle of chemicals and the cloth. "Perhaps a gentler approach might prevent future mishaps?"

"Thanks for the tip, but her life will be anything but gentle from here on out," he says. "I think we can handle her."

Galenia frowns up at the huge demon. Despite his rejection, she sets the bottle and cloth on Mara's stomach. "In case you change your mind," she says.

I think I see him shrug, but I could be mistaken. Without another word, he turns and carries his quarry back behind the black gate, and just like that, we are free of her.

TWENTY

Michaela

I hope to see the Fates out at the edge of the mists, but they aren't here. They must've left while I was talking to Ryker. A comforting hug would have been nice, but I don't really need it. This mission should be genuinely easy. There will be no witches waiting to jump out at me. No rogue Reapers who hope to kidnap me, or at least none who are unrestrained. On our last visit, there weren't even any ghosts wandering around, which leads me to believe Mara has some shield against them as well. Perhaps the dome serves more than one purpose.

As I walk through the mists, trying to stay focused on Shiloh, I see bits and pieces of his life, all happy moments with his mom and his friends. It seems like he had a good amount of friends, at least at one point in his life. There are a lot of happy memories even after he got sick. I see him at the hospital playing Go Fish with Nysa, and there's another memory of an elaborate prank he pulled on a poor, unsuspecting night nurse. It involved dumping glitter from a bedpan propped on his slightly open door. And so many happy moments with his mom. It's a strange dichotomy of the woman I know now, and the woman she was. Why didn't she cling to that? Anyone can see how happy she was. I sigh as I watch her pushing him on the swing and chasing him around the playground, the sound of his laughter filling the air around us. Maybe she was clinging to it. So tightly, in fact, she strangled all her happiness away.

I can't focus on her though. Instead, I turn my attention to him. His memories make me smile, preparing me well for a very satisfying reaping.

As the mists start to clear, I prepare myself for the long walk through the woods. But to my surprise, the dome is gone. The mists part in Mara's living room, bringing me as close to Shiloh as possible. I wonder if Nathair is still here. I'm tempted to go look for him, but I decide to leave him to the other Reapers. Shiloh is the one who needs me now.

A smile makes its way across my face as I realize I'm finally getting to do something I *want* to do. This child's life has been a misery ever since his thread reached its natural end, and I can finally bring him home.

I know this is right, and it makes me stand up a little straighter as I cross the short distance to the boy's room.

But while I'm excited to help Shiloh finally gain the peace that's eluded him for years, it's immediately clear he isn't happy to see me.

"You." His voice is quiet, and I barely hear him over the sound of the heart monitor. Once again, his soul is sitting in the chair next to the bed where his body lay struggling. "They sent *you* for me?"

"Yes. I felt it was a job I needed to finish."

"Are we nothing but jobs to you? My mom is a person. She's *my* mom. She doesn't deserve what is going to happen to her. What *is* going to happen to her?" Tears pool in his eyes.

I sit down in front of him, and for the first time, I touch him. As I scoop his hands into mine, the makeshift string connecting him to his body falls away and disappears. His heart monitor starts blaring alarms, but I ignore it. He is free.

He looks over at his body and knows it.

"Look at me, Shiloh." His eyes are wide when they meet mine. "I honestly don't know what is going to happen to your mother. I'm not sure what scenarios your mind has conjured, and I don't know if the truth is better or worse. I won't speculate. The problem is, she isn't sorry for what she did, for the lives she took. And you can't do things like that without facing consequences."

I try to make him see, but he doesn't. "Of course she isn't sorry. Don't you see? She was just trying to save her son, and it worked…sort of." He looks at the place where the string used to be tied around his wrist. Picking up his other hand, he rubs the spot, marveling at his freedom.

"No. This isn't right. Not at her expense." He clings to me, as if begging me to make it right.

"None of this is right," I say, giving him a sad look. "Your mother tampered with the way of things. With fate. While she 'saved' you for a time, you had no life. You merely existed. That was not supposed to be your fate. Your fate was to thrive in your short time on Earth. What you've been doing since she trapped you here isn't thriving. Frankly, she isn't succeeding either. She's actively destroying people."

"She was only trying to do what she thought was best for me."

I want to believe that, but in my heart, I know it isn't true. She was doing what she wanted. What she thought she needed, with no regard for what was best for her son or anyone else. But I can't say that to him.

"Life on Earth is full of a gamut of experiences, Shiloh, full of both joy and sorrow. Instead of feeling her sorrow, she chose to keep it at bay at a very high cost. If she'd allowed the future to unfold as was intended, you would have passed quickly and with minimal suffering. Instead, she took others' lives so you could linger here in pain. That's no way to exist."

The next time he speaks, he's filled with conviction. "I'd like to speak for her before she is punished."

"I don't know if that's possible, but I'll see what I can do," I concede.

When he's finally ready, we walk hand in hand to the mists. He stands tall as his home on Earth disappears behind us, and he finally reaches for his fate with outstretched arms.

The walk goes by in a blur. A part of me doesn't want this one to be over. If he gets his wish, if he's allowed to attend her trial, he'll be confronted head-on with what his mother did to keep him on Earth. And no child should have to contend with that. If nothing else, it makes my anger for Mara boil that much harder.

The gates of heaven appear, and a whole host of angels waits behind them, singing his name and welcoming him with open arms. It makes me smile that they pulled out all the stops for this little boy. He stops and watches them, and if it weren't for the way he's clinging to my hand, I'd think he was just taking it all in. But he's scared to cross this threshold.

"I can't go back once I go in there, can I?" he asks, although he already knows the answer.

"Shiloh, there was no going back long ago."

He takes a long, deep breath and lets me go. When he turns to face me, I don't see a sickly boy or a thin soul. I see a vibrant young boy, ready to go home.

Shiloh smiles at me, and it brings a rosy color to his cheeks.

"Thank you, Michaela," he says. Without warning, he throws his arms around me, and I fall flat on my butt from the force of it.

We laugh in a heap at the gates of heaven, with the angels singing all around us. One of them comes through and offers Shiloh a hand up. He looks at me, and I nod. He nods back, sure of himself now, and takes the angel's hand. I smile as I watch him disappear behind the gate, accompanied by his heavenly escort.

An angel comes and stands beside me, watching the spectacle too.

"He wants to be at the trial," I say.

"We know," she answers. Even when speaking, her voice is musical. I want to smile, although I don't know why.

"Can he?"

"No. It is too much to ask of a boy. No matter how old they

are, a child should not have to watch the demise of their parent. And no matter what is decided today, one way or another, Mara will be facing her demise."

"Today?" I ask, turning to face the golden-haired angel beside me.

"Now."

TWENTY-ONE

Penn

After the Guardians take Mara away, the three of us don't really know what to do with ourselves. Not until someone emerges from the golden gate to greet us.

It's Miette again. She's beaming from ear to year. Bounding over to us like a young deer, she throws her arms around my waist and squeezes with all her might.

"You did it! You saved her."

She pulls back from her embrace and looks up at me, still bubbling over with joy. "Ryker wants to see you." She adds it like some kind of aside. Like it means nothing.

"What do you mean? Just me?"

"He asked for the one dressed as a Keeper. I assume that's you."

When I glance at my sister Fates, I see a reflection of the fear I feel in my own heart.

"What?" She shrugs. "Don't let Ryker intimidate you. He's a big softie once you get to know him. Just stay on his good side and you'll be fine." She smiles up at me. When my expression doesn't change, she reaches out and squeezes my arm, forcing me to look down at her.

"I promise. After saving one of Ryker's favorite Reapers, you'll be on his good side for a long time."

I swallow hard, and she smiles at me. "Come on. He won't bite, I swear."

But I'm not so sure. Why would he want to see me, and only me, unless he knows who I am? If he just wanted to say thank you, he'd have asked for all of us.

I think back to the last time I saw him. It was in Michaela's healing room after we got back from hell. Ryker came to see her. He spoke briefly to me, and I thought I caught a sparkle in his eye. He made some quip about Michaela's curious friends. But he didn't seem all that surprised that a Keeper was paying her a visit.

It wasn't enough to confirm or deny whether he knew my true identity.

Miette leads the way through the gate and down the hallway to the Reapers' wing. My sisters cling to my hands as we make our way to what feels like my end.

When we reach Ryker's door, Galenia and Horatia come to a stop just behind me. I turn to face them.

"I love you both. Please tell Michaela..." I trail off. What message could truly explain how I feel? My gratitude. My love for her.

"We will," Galenia says with shining eyes.

"Save Kismet and the others for me, will you? Tell them I'm sorry. Make sure they are taken care of."

"We will," Horatia says, her voice thick with emotion.

They throw their arms around me one last time, and with that, I'm left to face my fate.

———————

"Ah. Michaela's dear friend. I was wondering when I'd be seeing you," Ryker says as I come through the door with a bit of hesitation. He's sitting behind a huge white desk, perfectly accented by the black cabinets to his left and black bookshelves to his right.

He gestures to a white armchair in front of him. There's a black velvet one next to it, and I wonder if Michaela has ever sat in one of these chairs. "Please, have a seat. I've sent Michaela to retrieve Shiloh. We have some matters to discuss while she's gone."

I sink into the chair, but I try to avoid eye contact with the huge man across the desk from me. He doesn't make it easy. But while his presence is naturally intimidating, I can tell he's trying to set me at ease. Why? Is he leading me into a trap? I'm grateful to my hood, although I know it offers me little in the way of actual protection.

"I've never spent so much time among the Fates before. I'm starting to like you folks," he says with a smile on his face.

Despite the fact that his smile isn't sinister in any way, it doesn't put me at ease. He's confirmed it; he knows who I am. It's over. My last shred of hope that he might have asked me here to thank me for saving Michaela is gone. A thousand thoughts run through my mind, and I wonder if this is what a human means when they say their life flashed before their eyes. I think of the time I spent on Earth with Andrew and Kismet, of Galenia and Horatia, my soul's sisters, and of Michaela, whom I won't get to see again.

Ryker sits back in his chair and waves a hand at me. "I've called you here for a reason, but it isn't to doom you."

I relax, but only a little. Why? What's his motivation? I shake myself a little. My time on Earth has made me think too much like a human. Malice isn't something that flows as freely in the heavens as it does on Earth. Ryker isn't out to get me. He's a heavenly being, and a boss at that. If he wanted me gone, I'd already be vapor. He trusts Michaela, so he must trust me.

Of course, that doesn't mean I'm comfortable. The more people who know I'm here, the more danger I'm in. It will only take one soul with that information to destroy me.

Taking a deep breath, I pull my hood away from my face, putting all my cards out on the table. He knows who I am, so there's no sense in being uncomfortable.

"Fine, Ryker. What do you want?" It comes out cold, which isn't what I intended. I suppose I'm just steeling myself for whatever he's going to say next.

"Now, now. No need to be so defensive. I promise that I do not intend to harm you." He leans forward in his chair. "Michaela has asked to help retrieve the remaining humans captured in the prison of souls. You will accompany her. Most likely after Mara's trial is over. In the meantime, I've sent emissaries ahead of her to make sure the souls are safe and your path to them will be clear."

I let out a deep breath. They will be okay. They'll be taken care of. No matter what.

He reaches for something to his left, and I grip the sides of the armchair for dear life.

It's a roll of parchment with a gold seal on it.

"I've been asked to give you this."

He holds it out to me, and I hesitantly accept it. The parchment is new and crisp. The seal has a hand on it. The hand of God. I swallow hard.

"What is this?"

Ryker smiles mischievously at me. "How should I know? Open it and see."

Throwing caution to the wind, I crack the seal and unfurl the scroll.

The writing is perfect calligraphy, written in gold ink.

This document hereby serves as a full and complete pardon to the former Fate and Spinner, Penn.

There's a personal note down below, written in a rather messy hand.

Penn,
I owe you my eternal thanks. You have made me proud. Do whatever you wish with your pardon. You may choose to stay here among the heavens, or perhaps you would rather return to Earth. Opportunities will present themselves soon. Choose however you wish. But above all, choose happiness.
—G

"I…" I'm speechless. I'm pardoned. Safe. My anxieties have

suddenly been lifted off my shoulders—a one-hundred-pound weight I didn't realize I was bearing. I sit up straighter, smile broader, and take a deep, cleansing breath.

"Not so fast, my friend. Your work here still isn't finished. Michaela tells me those souls are still stuck in hell. You can't just abandon them to go flitting off through the fields of Earth like some country bumpkin." He says it with a glint in his eye, and I know he's teasing me.

"I have no intention of abandoning them."

He leans back in his chair and smiles. "Yes, indeed. You Fates aren't half bad at all."

Reaching across the desk, he extends an arm to me, and we shake hands in a brotherly fashion. "Thank you for returning her to us." His voice is low and full of gratitude. It seems I owe him a fair amount of thanks as well, but he doesn't allow me to speak again.

"Now, we have a trial to get to."

———————

We are seated in a U-shaped room with auditorium-style seating that climbs several stories high. We Fates are seated high up, near the left tip of the U. The walls and floor are white, but the seats are a beautiful golden color, lined with plush cushions to keep us comfortable while we wait.

Despite the fact that it's the middle of the workday, it seems as though everything has come to a halt for this moment. As I look out across the rows and rows of seats, it seems as if all the heavens, and some of hell, have come to see this human and what will become of her. I don't see many empty seats, that's for sure. The one I have saved for Michaela is one of the last empties in the room.

There are several different kinds of demons pacing around the floor below us, waiting for Mara to be brought in. I'm not sure what they all are. Michaela would have been able to identify them. For about the hundredth time, I find myself searching for her amidst the seated Reapers. I wonder how she did with Shiloh, and if she's doing okay. I know this will be a bittersweet reaping for her.

Suddenly, the door at the base of the U bursts open, revealing Michaela. She's out of breath, much as she was when she came rushing into the weaving room just a short time ago to tell me about the prison of souls. So much has happened since then.

I whistle at Michaela as she scans the seats. She spots me and waves. But then she spies the other Reapers, Ryker among them, and a dilemma plays out on her face when her boss waves her over. The head Reaper saves her. He motions for her to sit with us and nods, clearly assuring her it's all right. She smiles and waves gratefully at him before making her way toward us.

She's still out of breath when she plops down next to me. Horatia and Galenia smile and wave at her from their seats opposite me. Michaela leans over and says, "Shiloh wanted to come. To speak for her."

"What? Are they going to let him?" I ask, keeping my eyes up front.

"No." It's a simple word, but I can tell she's of two minds about their decision.

My eyes are focused at the back of the room, so it takes me by surprise when a door opens in the middle of the top of the U-shaped room. God comes out, and a low roar spreads throughout the room. I turn away from the back of the room just in time to see Him take a seat behind a gold desk atop a white platform that runs the length of the top of the U.

"I didn't know there was a door back there, did you?" I ask, bewildered.

"Nope. I've never been in this room before," Michaela answers as she takes another quick look around. The room really is a spectacle to behold.

God clears his throat, and the murmuring ceases abruptly. "Thank you all for coming. Bring in the accused." He says it while looking down at some papers. His glasses are perched at the end of His nose, and He's dressed in a white suit with a gold tie.

My sentencing was different, that's for sure. He was basically dressed in jeans and a shirt for that. There wasn't this fancy gold seating either. But this is so much more serious than the trial of some lovesick Fate. Mara might be one human, but she's left a trail of pain and broken people behind her.

With a rush of air, the doors at the back of the room open, admitting two huge demons. They're pitch black, with horns that curve down toward their mouths. Their red eyes scan the room as they tightly grip huge sledgehammers.

"Hunters. I wonder why they're here," Michaela whispers.

"You fought one of *those* in hell?" I ask in shock. "They're huge!" The enormous demons are locking eyes with the people in the first row of balcony seating. Suddenly, I'm glad we're in the top tier.

"Yes. Shush," she says as she watches the scene intently, craning to see behind the Hunters.

A small human follows a few paces behind them. *Her*. She's draped in flaming chains that clang as she walks. Her hands are completely covered with solid black iron cuffs, leaving no room for a swish of the hand or a flick of the finger.

She doesn't seem to be in any pain from the flames that are roaring all around her. Rather, she follows the Hunters with a stiff back and her chin held high.

I recognize the demons behind her as Guardians. Six of them. They know what they're dealing with here and aren't taking any chances. I can't help but wonder what she did during her short tenure in hell to make them change their tune about her. The Guardian we left her with seemed so confident.

They file down the center of the room, and the silent, heavy air fills with the fiery crackle of Mara's chains and the percussive thump of the demon's footsteps. I feel like the entire room is holding its breath as they make their way toward God.

Once they reach the base of the platform, the two Hunters part, and Mara steps forward. The six Guardians form a rectangular barrier around her, with the Hunters at the head of it.

In the silence, I hear a whisper that turns to a song. My blood goes cold, and I stand up like a shot. "She's at it again. She's going to attack Him!"

My voice echoes in the large room, and almost everyone

turns to look at me. Even the huge demons.

Michaela pulls on my arm, urging me to sit back down. "Trust Him. It will be okay."

But I can't bring myself to sit. I stand there, watching as her song creates a blue sliver of fog that snakes around the demons. Slowly, people follow my pointing finger and turn back toward the human. I can't begin to understand what she's trying to accomplish. Maybe she just doesn't want to go down without a fight.

The long, blue shape snakes around the Hunters, but instead of panicking, they smile at each other. Just as it's making its way around their hammers, they bring them down hard, making a thunderous sound that echoes throughout the huge room.

On instinct, I sit back down in my chair, mouth open, waiting to see what will happen next.

The two Hunters turn to Mara and laugh. "Anything else?"

Mara says nothing, but I swear I can see her standing a little straighter. There's an unmistakable air of defiance about her.

The edges of God's face are drawn down by the weight of what she's done, what she continues to do, as He watches her.

"So, Mara. You choose to fight, even now." It's not a question, and I think I hear her scoff at Him. I didn't make her that bold when I spun her. Once again, I find myself wondering how she strayed so far. I frown down at her and can't help but shake my head.

"Of course I continue to fight. I will always fight against You. You've taken everything from me."

He winces. "I have given you everything. I gave you the powers you have, and yet you turn them against me?"

"Horse shit," she says. As if on cue, a collective gasp rings throughout the room. "Oh, get over yourselves," she says. "I learned most of these skills on my own, without any help from You or anyone."

Then she does the unthinkable. She spits at the feet of God. "At any rate, I don't care about that. You can have my powers, or whatever you want to call them. You took away my mother, my grandmother, my husband. I'm not letting you take my baby."

Michaela shifts in discomfort. She's already taken Mara's son to heaven. And Mara doesn't know.

God looks our direction and makes eye contact with Michaela. She smiles softly at Him; he nods in return, as if thanking her for the part she's played.

"Your son is already home. He's with his father and grandparents now."

An otherworldly scream fills the room. It starts out low, growing until I'm forced to cover my ears. Michaela jumps to standing; she looks like she's ready to leap over the seats to face the human. We've all seen what Mara can do, and now she really has nothing to lose.

God doesn't so much as fidget as Mara continues to shriek. As the sound goes on, something shocking happens. The Guardian directly behind her starts to glow. The cracks in his skin blaze brighter and brighter until he explodes. Black shards go flying everywhere.

When I turn to look at Michaela, she's already three rows down from us. I can't see how she's doing it, but she's scaling the rows. She'll never make it to the bottom, but I can see she wants to try.

Two other Guardians explode, one after another, and flaming shrapnel hits a few of the angels down front. Chaos is starting to unfold. At least twenty Archangels flood the floor, racing to help the demons get the human under control, but my eyes are on Michaela. She's jumped to the second tier of seating at this point and is making her way closer to the bottom.

Through it all, God sits calmly at his desk, not reacting to the chaos unfolding around Him.

It's hard to see from this distance, but I swear Mara's eyes have turned red, as if the flames within her soul are about to come pouring out. She's opening her mouth again—for another shriek?—as Michaela makes her way down the first tier. My friend has nearly reached the floor when Mara spews actual fire at the remaining three Guardians.

The Hunters have turned with their backs to God, as if to protect Him, although I can't imagine that's their primary purpose. The Guardians scramble, trying to maintain their tenuous grasp on the upper hand.

Suddenly, I'm struck by the odd scene unfolding in front of me. Never before have I seen angels and demons fight a common enemy. Together. Mara's evil is so absolute, even the demons know she's bad news.

Panic suddenly takes hold of me. Michaela's down there with that woman who has singlehandedly destroyed so many heavenly beings.

"*Michaela*," I scream at the top of my lungs, but she's much too far away to hear me. I lurch forward, but Horatia grabs hold of my arm.

"It's too late," she shouts above the noise.

Souls are scattering, no longer interested in what happens to this woman. They just want out, away from their potential doom, and I don't really blame them. The scene unfolding in front of us is unprecedented.

"Mara!" Michaela's voice pierces its way through the racket, and my stomach lurches. She is standing on the floor just behind the human, with flames roaring all around her. In fact, I think the bottom of her gown is ablaze. The need to call out to her, to help her, to stomp out her fiery hem is almost unbearable. I don't want to watch her disintegrate. I can't bear to witness that. But I also can't tear my eyes away from her.

Mara turns around slowly. She's breathing heavily, and I can tell her rage has not been satisfied. I wonder if there's even anything left of the human I created so long ago.

Everyone who's still in the room stops and stares at her, captivated by her mania.

"You," she says, her iron-capped hands dangling by her sides. "You're the one responsible for taking my son, aren't you?"

Michaela stands up straighter. Without taking her eyes off Mara, she says, "Yes, I am." Despite the fact that she didn't shout it, her answer echoes around the room.

"And now you've come here for what? To see the end of me? Or to see the end of *you*?" Her tone is sinister, but Michaela doesn't shy away.

"No," I breathe, and Horatia grabs my hand so tightly her nails dig into my palm.

Mara's smile is a sickening promise of death, destruction, and pain, but Michaela doesn't shy away from her. I'm watching them so closely that I almost miss the Hunter that is creeping up behind Mara. He reaches around in front of her and slaps a piece of black iron over her mouth. It clamps shut in the back and trails a fiery chain similar to the ones draped over her body.

"That's enough out of you," the Hunter says. He shifts his gaze to Michaela. "You owe me one."

Michaela can only look up at the huge demon and nod. I can't believe she faced one of those alone in hell and won. She still has yet to tell me that whole story. I remind myself to ask her about it when this is finally over.

Michaela turns to face God with what's left of the demons. The angels are battered, but they stand tall with her. Angels and demons move closer together, as if they are comrades. I suppose in this one instance, they are.

God sighs, and the weight of the disappointment emanating from Him is crushing. I almost don't have the will to bring my eyes up to Mara.

"You leave me with no choice, Mara," He says, still not looking at her. When He finally raises His eyes, I know this is it. In slow motion, I watch him look down at her as he lowers his gavel. "You are sentenced to extinction."

Simultaneous roars and gasps erupt in the room, making it hard to know if God said anything else.

Never, in all my centuries as a Fate, have I heard of such a thing. Even Hitler went to hell. This is beyond anything I've ever expected, but after seeing her in action just now, I can't say I'm surprised. I'm not sure they could contain her in hell. Sure, they'd love the challenge, but if she got away from them, we'd be right back where we started, maybe worse.

When the commotion dies down, God speaks again. "You, Mara, will not be granted a home in heaven with your son. Nor will you be allowed to continue on in hell. Instead, you will cease to exist."

The demons raise their voices in outrage. "You're *stealing* her from us," one of the Hunters shouts in a booming voice.

"She *belongs* to us," the second Hunter adds.

"While that would be true under normal circumstances, I'm sorry to say this case is unique."

A small Guardian steps forward, moving between Mara and God. "Perhaps if you separate her from her body, she would be more manageable, if you get my meaning."

The demon makes an interesting proposition.

"Why not try it?" he continues. "If it doesn't work, you can still eliminate her, no harm done."

God is silent for a few moments, seeming to consider the option. "No," he finally says. "I will not endanger more of my creations. Not even you, Guardian. Mara is beyond any of us. Even me. This ends here and now."

With His word, she slowly begins to fade. Her eyes grow wide with surprise, but there is nothing she can do. With her mouth covered by the metal band, we don't even hear her scream. She just becomes more and more opaque, until she isn't there at all.

TWENTY-TWO

Michaela

I don't believe it. She disappeared right before my eyes. Despite the fact that I've seen her destroy plenty of heavenly beings that way, it's awful to see it happen to a human, a live, flesh and blood creature. But then I think of what she did to Webber and reconsider.

My heart is broken for everyone we've lost since all this started. But just as my knees are about to give out, depositing me in the very spot where she disappeared, God addresses me.

"Michaela. *Diligence.* Your work is not yet done." I'm torn between screaming at Him and taking strength from His words. Haven't I done enough?

I did ask to be the one to free the remaining prisoners from hell. Ryker agreed to my request, and I can't back down now, particularly not from His commands. Even though I want to collapse into a weeping puddle in the middle of this room, surrounded by demons, I straighten my back, stiffen my bottom lip, and nod.

With a simple tilt of my head, I turn and walk out of the room. Although I just walked in a few minutes ago, I'm somehow a different woman. I'm stronger, but more broken too. It's a strength I will need to cling to for the journey ahead, back into hell.

Penn, Horatia, and Galenia meet me at the door. They are ready too. I can't tell them no. They're in this as much as I am. They deserve to see this through to the end, especially Penn. He needs this.

Together, we head to the black gate. With any luck, this will be the last time we make this trip as a group.

At first, we don't talk, but after a while, I can't take the silence anymore. "I can't believe she just disappeared like that."

"It's no more than she deserved," Penn says as we make our way across the clouds. There's a hint of bitterness in his voice. He's frowning deeply as he stomps toward the black gate, which hasn't even appeared yet.

Before I can respond, he changes his tune. His expression softens. "I'm not sure I mean that. I do…but then again, I don't. I guess you were right. I'm glad I didn't have to be the one to decide her fate."

He doesn't look at me when he says it, just keeps walking on ahead.

I hang back far enough so Penn can't hear us and wrap my arms around Horatia and Galenia. "What's wrong with him?" I whisper.

"Oh, a little of this, a little of that," Horatia answers mysteriously.

Galenia smiles at me and offers a little more. "Now that this is over, or at least almost over, the full gravity of everything that's happened is hitting him. He was so focused on reacting, I don't think he let himself fully understand what had been taken from Andrew and Kismet and the others. I think he's feeling angry right now."

"Well, that much is clear." He's stomping off to the left, but he's headed in the wrong direction. I let him go a little further as the black gates form in front of me. He needs to bleed off some of his anger before we go into a place that feeds on that emotion.

I don't try to comfort him. There's nothing I can say. My own heart is tired too. But the finish line is in sight; it's just behind the black gates. Penn hasn't noticed they've materialized yet. He's still pacing around near the edge of the mists.

"Do you think we should call him over?" Horatia asks as we hesitate at the gate, waiting for our wayward Fate.

"No. Let him work through it," I say, watching him. His head is down, and he's kicking at something invisible. "It's reaching its peak." It will boil over soon; I can feel it.

And it does. He cries out, his screams swallowed by the mists, and falls to his knees. When I reach him, there are tears streaming down his face. His sisters are there too, but he's looking at me.

"After this, I'll never see her again."

His broken heart is pulverizing mine, and I go to my knees in front of him, taking his hands in mine. Tears stream down my own face, until we're both just a couple of blubbering idiots at the edge of the mists. I'm thankful no one is coming or going at the moment.

He holds out his arms to me and I fall into them, savoring the warmth that surrounds me. In that moment, we are broken together. And maybe our broken pieces can be put back together to make something new when this is all over. That hope gives me the strength to stand up. He follows, never letting go of my hand.

"Let's go," he says, taking Horatia's hand in his free one. She nods and links hands with Galenia. Our chain of heavenly souls marches toward the black gate more confidently than the last two times we crossed this threshold together.

"Ryker sent emissaries ahead of us. It should be easy this time. No fuss. No muss." I'm saying it for myself as much as I'm saying it for them.

No one is waiting for us at the gate, which doesn't surprise me. We don't have a scheduled delivery, after all. Once we're all on the other side, we stand there for a moment, steeling ourselves to face whatever's ahead. I don't imagine it will be anything like the death-defying journey Penn and I faced the last time we were here, but it's still not something I would *choose* to do. Being in hell is just that—it's hell.

So, after taking a deep breath, I start walking toward the prison.

"I don't know about you guys, but I'd like to get in and out of here as quickly as possible." I don't look back to see if they're following me. I know they are.

But we don't get very far. A group of demons is waiting for us.

"Well, hello. We meet again." It's the same demon who took Webber. I bristle.

"Hello. What can I do for you?"

"We thought we'd have a little celebration here in hell. The human was destroyed, and we're about to lose three other inmates to you folks, but why not live it up, huh? Would you like to join us?" His voice is sinister, and his words don't give me a warm, fuzzy feeling.

"Thank you for your generosity, but I think we'll just collect the souls from their prison and go." I try to push past him, but he won't let me.

"Now, now, Reaper. We're trying to show you some hospitality. Don't be so quick to reject it." His tone changes to a warning on that last sentence, giving me goose bumps.

"I was assured we would be allowed safe entry and passage. Are you purposefully delaying us?"

"What?" He puts a hand on his chest, feigning injury. "Why, we simply thought you might like some respite, maybe some refreshments, after such a difficult few days. No one can party like us demons."

"I believe you on that one," Horatia says, just loud enough for us to hear her.

The demon looks at her and smiles. "I remember you. The fast learner. I take it you don't trust me?"

She snorts, and he smiles wider. "Rightfully so," he says before turning back to me. "Listen, Reaper, we can do this the easy way, or the hard way. Both will take you more time than you want. You're in my territory now. You'll play by my rules."

"Oh, will I?" I say, taking a step toward the demon and wiping that glowing grin right off his face. "How about I march back to my superiors and tell them what's going on here? That *you* won't let me near the prison. That I'm unable to retrieve what's rightfully ours."

He straightens at that. He's at least a head taller than I am, but I don't cower the way he expects. I scowl at him. Then a huge shadow appears behind the demon. The demon gives me a toothy grin and steps aside to make way for the Hunter from the trial. He takes a few steps toward me. He's so huge it's enough to close the distance between us.

"Reaper. I didn't expect to see you again so soon."

"I'm here for the souls in the prison."

He nods. "Well, don't let me stop you. I believe you know the way." He tips his head down and gives me a half smile, as if the two of us have a bond. After what happened at the sentencing, I think maybe we do.

"What?" the smaller demon booms.

The Hunter turns to him. "What?" He's asking in earnest. He doesn't understand why the demon has a problem with that plan.

"You're just going to let her take them?" He puffs out his chest and takes a step toward the Hunter. I don't see the hammer anywhere, but I'm pretty sure he doesn't need it to squash the smaller demon.

"And you're not?" The demon doesn't answer, so the Hunter follows up with another question. "And what were you going to do with those souls? Take them dancing?"

"Well, I certainly wasn't going to make it easy for them. Isn't that our job?" He's whining now, and it's even more grating than his normal voice.

The Hunter takes a half step toward the demon and towers over him. "Speaking of work, don't you have souls to torture?"

To my disbelief, the demon doesn't back down. As they say on Earth, he has some cojones. He glances over and catches me smiling.

"What are *you* smiling at, Reaper?" He spits out my title.

"You. I'm smiling at you, and the fact that you actually think you can win this."

The Hunter turns on me. "Let's get one thing straight, *Reaper*," he growls. "You and I are not on the same team."

"Noted," I say. So much for our bond.

He turns back to the demon.

"You see that?" the smaller demon whines. "She's so full of herself; she actually thought you were her ally. I think we should take her down a peg or two. Just like that Fate we had down here for a bit."

"That what?" he asks, and the demon clamps his mouth shut. "I was told he was a delusional human the Reapers had misplaced. He was truly a Spinner?"

The demon clears his throat. "Why do you care anyway? Besides, you're a Hunter. I don't answer to you."

"That's true, you don't." A Warden creeps out of the shadows, and I stifle a groan.

Although the Warden has a small, unassuming appearance, he's the one I dread most. Well, after the Hunter. They're manipulative, which makes them particularly dangerous, and they oversee the torture of the souls who are kept here. Just the sight of him turns my stomach, and I feel an overwhelming need to leave.

"But the Hunter's right. That *is* the story you told everyone. Why change it now?" he asks the demon, without even acknowledging us. I'm fine with that.

The demon takes a step back for the first time since he approached us. I stay silent this time, taking care to control my expression as I watch the downfall of the demon who trapped Webber.

"The punishment for knowingly trapping a heavenly soul here is severe. But you know that, don't you?" His voice is low and soothing as he slowly walks toward the demon. The demon continues to back away.

The Hunter stays put, watching with the rest of us as the Warden backs the demon into the darkness. Part of me is a little sad that I won't see what becomes of him. But another part of me is grateful to be spared the details. I don't need to witness any more brutality. I've seen enough to last me forever, really.

Once the other demons "partying" with him have dispersed, I find myself standing next to the Hunter, peering into the darkness. Clearing my throat, I turn to the hulking demon. "Hunter."

"Reaper." We nod at each other, and he goes back the way he came, leaving the Fates and me alone again.

"Well, that was interesting," Penn says as we make our way toward the prison of souls.

"Things are always interesting on this side of the black gate," I say as we make our way down skull-lined hallways lit with an eerie red glow.

"Let's just get the souls and get out of here," Horatia says, walking with her arms clutched around her body.

"Agreed," I say, picking up the pace a little bit.

A few twists and turns later, we're all standing at the door to the prison. I trace the circular symbol of flowing waves with my finger.

"Are you gonna go in?" Horatia asks, but Penn is hesitating too. He knows how hard this will be.

"Once we go in, we say goodbye to them," I say.

"Isn't that a good thing?" Galenia asks. "They're going home. Where they belong."

It's exactly what I needed to hear. "You're right." I take a deep breath, but before I push the door open, I turn toward the woman who's helped lead me through all this madness. "You know, you would've been a good Reaper, Galenia."

She laughs, and we can't help but smile with her. "I don't think so. I daydream too much."

Chuckling, I concede. "Maybe."

Then there's nothing left to do but push the door open and see what awaits us inside the prison of souls.

Thankfully, all three souls are inside. No one has disappeared. No one has succumbed to a worse fate. However, Andrew looks close to giving up. He's only a shadow of his former self.

They lift their heads at once, cowering reflexively. "I know you," Lily says from the back corner. "You said you'd save me." My heart breaks, but I can't take my eyes off Andrew. He's so weak; he can't do more than lift his head to look at us.

Horatia goes to him first, trying to free him from his shackles.

"The key. Michaela, where is the key?" she demands.

I glance at the little hook on the wall, but it isn't there. Kismet speaks up in a voice hoarse from either crying or disuse. "It's on the floor. Over there."

She nods her head to the left. Sure enough, there it is. I remember now. We were in such a hurry to get out of here last time, Penn just threw the key down and we ran.

Horatia retrieves it and hurriedly frees Andrew. "What's happening to him?" she asks.

"He's wasting away," I say, watching as Penn frees Kismet, waiting for the key so I can release Lily from her bindings. She looks frightened, and rightfully so. I kneel down in front of her.

"It's going to be okay now. You're safe."

"I'm not safe. Not in here. Do you *know* where we are?" She whispers it at me, as if saying the word out loud might make it more real.

"I know. But your time here is over. I'm taking you home for good."

"He's wasting away?" Horatia asks.

I sigh. I can't juggle these important conversations. "Penn, can you help me out here?"

But he's too focused on Kismet. She's not as far gone as Andrew, but she doesn't look good either. Lily hasn't been here as long as they have. She's basically unaffected, save for a sheer and utter terror of her surroundings.

"This place, it's bad for those who don't belong," I say to Horatia as I free Lily. "We need to get him into the healing rooms. Then he can go home. To be honest, I think they both need some time in the healing rooms." I'm hoping it will be enough to bring the sparkle back to Kismet's eyes.

Horatia is standing with Andrew's arm slung over her shoulders. He's totally limp against her and his feet drag lifelessly behind him. Souls do not weigh anything, thankfully, and Horatia can manage him easily. As Penn scoops Kismet into his arms, I hold my hand out to Lily.

"How can I trust you, after what happened last time?" she asks, looking up at me with fearful eyes. "You were supposed to keep me safe."

Hearing those words again pulverizes the pieces of my broken heart into powder. "I'm so sorry, Lily."

Galenia is at my side at once. "Lily, my sweet child," she says in a soft tone. "She *is* saving you. She just needed some help. We're all going to take you home now. You'll never have to see the inside of this horrible place again. We promise."

I glance at Penn and Horatia, but they're too preoccupied with the souls they're helping. "I think we should go. Now," Horatia says.

"Go on ahead, Ratia. We'll be right behind you," Galenia says, and I'm so grateful for her. Some souls need more of a talking to, and she gets that.

I look at Penn, and he nods to me. Kismet puts her head on his shoulder, and I can see how much he's hurting by the stricken look on his face. But he turns and carries her out of the prison for good, just as he should.

I turn to Lily and give her my full attention. "I'm so sorry I couldn't save you that day. But Galenia is right. I never stopped trying to get to you. The woman who did this to you is gone. And she's never coming back. It's over. We can walk out of here as soon as you're ready, and I will take you home."

"Walk out of here? Do you know what's out there?" she says, bringing her knees up and wrapping her arms around them. She buries her face in the nest she's made and only peeks out with her eyes, which are partially hidden by long, brown bangs.

"I do know what's out there. But I'm not afraid." I can't think of anything else to say that will comfort her. *You'll be safe,*

I promise, won't work. She thought that the last time. I start to wonder if another Reaper should have come here to collect her.

No. I started this, and it's up to me to finish it. I sit down next to Lily, and Galenia takes my cue and sits on the other side. She's tucked in a safe little cocoon between us.

"What's your favorite song, Lily?" I ask her.

"I don't know. There are lots." The question changes her whole demeanor. It's like we've lit a spark within her.

"I like Taylor Swift and Adele. And Bruno Mars. A bunch of my friends like Justin Bieber, but I'm not much of a boy-band person. I don't like his music. He's not a very good singer." She shrugs.

"Well, Galenia, what do you think? Should we sing 'Shake it off' or 'Hello' or 'Just the Way You Are'?"

Instead of answering me, she starts singing in a soft, melodious voice. Then she stands up and starts dancing to the tune. Galenia will never cease to surprise me. "*I stay out too late...*"

I get up and join her, singing along to the song I barely know. We laugh, and Lily fills in the parts we're not so sure about. Soon, the three of us are dancing around together, singing our hearts out in the middle of the prison of souls. I know without a doubt this is the only happiness this place has ever seen.

When the song is done, we collapse in a heap of laughter, breathing hard.

"Okay. Let's go," Lily says with her head on my lap.

"Okay. Let's go," I say, smiling at Galenia, sending her a silent thank you. She squeezes my hand as we get up, and we walk hand in hand with Lily, leaving the prison of souls completely empty.

TWENTY-THREE

Penn

The sight of Kismet takes my breath away. Horatia is saying something about Andrew, but I only have eyes for her. Her spark is totally gone, leaving behind this opaque shell. Her hair is lackluster and matted in places, while her face is stained with tears. And her beautiful green eyes have gone dull, as if hope never existed there at all.

It's the most heartbreaking thing I've ever seen.

I fall to my knees in front of her, waiting impatiently for Horatia to free Andrew. She's struggling with the old lock, working hard to get it to engage. After what seems like an eternity, Andrew falls forward into her, no longer held up by his own arms.

The key falls to the ground, but she's too busy trying to get Andrew on his feet to stoop and pick it up.

I scramble to get it and bring it back to Kismet. Horatia is asking a question, and Michaela is talking to the little girl, but I can't absorb what's going on around me. All I can see is Kismet. We should've come back sooner. Maybe skipped the trial. We should've done something to get them out of here.

But there's no point in revisiting the decisions we made in

the past. We're here now, and that's what matters. She'll be okay, but only if we leave *now*. I finally look away from her to check on Andrew. He's far worse off than Kismet.

"We should go," I say quietly to Horatia after scooping Kismet into my arms. I nod toward Andrew.

"I think we should go. Now," Horatia confirms, and Michaela finally looks over. She's totally preoccupied with the child. The little girl is free, but she's sort of cowering by the wall.

Galenia turns and tells us to go on ahead, and I'm so grateful for that.

Without our Reaper, I anticipate being stopped more than once by the demons meandering through the halls of hell. But they leave us alone. They must know who we are, or maybe they know the souls we carry do not belong here. Either way, they do nothing more than glare at us. It makes me uneasy, but I'll take it.

Once we reach the outskirts of hell, in sight of the gate, Horatia stops ahead of me. I quicken my steps to catch up with her, dread tightening around my heart. Is something wrong with Andrew? Is he not going to make it?

"What's up?"

She lets Andrew go, and miracle of miracles, he stands. Smiling weakly, he holds out his hand. He's reaching for Kismet. I look down at the beautiful soul in my arms. I made them for each other, and it shows in the way she's looking at him, her eyes full of such devotion and love.

Slowly, I set her down on her feet, taking care to make sure she can stand on her own. Frankly, I have no idea how Andrew is doing it. He's so far gone that I can see the gate right through him.

He takes her hand, and it's as if a switch has been flipped. He's so much more vibrant. His smile grows wider, and the smallest hint of a sparkle returns to his eyes. To hers. Like maybe hope *didn't* die in that horrible prison.

Watching them, I know it's the first time they've touched in a very long time. Something catches in my throat, and I cough to clear it.

Andrew doesn't notice. "I thought we should walk out of

here together."

"I couldn't agree more," Kismet says, and they slowly walk toward the gate.

Horatia hooks her arm in mine and we follow behind, close enough to catch them if they lose their strength, but far enough away to give them some privacy.

As I watch them together, my heart is made whole again, even if it means saying goodbye to the only humans I have ever truly loved.

———

When the gate closes behind us, I can't help but yelp for joy. The sudden sound startles my friends, but I'm so happy. Taking Horatia in my arms, I spin her around. Andrew and Kismet laugh as they watch us.

After a little while, I settle down enough to go to my human friends, holding my hands out in congratulations.

"Now what?" Andrew asks.

"I think you should go to a healer, my friend. You need to be whole again."

He looks at Kismet. "I *am* whole."

Somehow, I knew that's what his answer would be, but I persist. "You'll be more comfortable in the long run if you just spend a day with the healers, Andrew. You'll be better for it."

"And what about Kismet?"

"She can go with you. She could use a little R and R."

"I'll rest when we're home," Kismet says.

"I understand. I'm sure you'll be perfectly comfortable together in heaven."

Reluctantly, I lead the way across the clouds to heaven's gates. We don't have a Reaper with us, so I'm not sure they'll appear, but the angels must sense their quarry because the gates appear in all their sparkling brilliance. Stopping in front of them, I turn to face Kismet and Andrew.

"I just want to say one thing, before…" I trail off. Before what? Before I never see them again? Before it's too late? "Well, anyway, before I lose my chance. I…"

THE HUMAN

It's harder than I thought it would be. How do you translate your heart into words so the people standing across from you might understand you a little better? I shift my weight and they all stare at me, even Horatia. I look to her for strength, and she gives me a small, encouraging smile.

Taking a deep breath, I start again. "I wanted to say I'm sorry. To both of you. Nearly everything that's happened is my fault. I should never have interfered. And for that, I am deeply sorry." I hang my head, unable to make eye contact with either of them, and wait for their response. Honestly, I don't really expect them to say anything. They only have eyes for each other now, and part of me thinks they'll walk right past me into heaven, where they'll live happily ever after.

But they don't. In fact, my head jerks up at the sound of Andrew laughing. "Oh, get over yourself, Penn," he says and claps a hand on my shoulder. I don't feel its weight, but I can see it there, barely. "Mara would've done what she did whether you were there to 'interfere' or not." He uses air quotes around the word interfere. "And if you hadn't been there, Kismet would have been alone after Mara took me."

He holds out his hand for me, and I take it. We shake as brothers, and my heart lurches with the knowledge of how much I will miss him.

"Penn, I have one question for you," Kismet says, and I turn to face her. Being free of hell for less than half an hour has been good for her. The color is already returning to her face, and her eyes are regaining some of their brilliance. I want to take her face in my hands and hug her like I'll never hug her again. Because I won't.

"Why me? Why us? Nysa knew Mara, and Jeff knew Nysa, so it stands to reason that she led Mara to him. But the rest of us seemed to be random. Why us?"

It's something I've been thinking about for a long time. Why Andrew? Why Kismet? At first, I thought it had something to do with me, that it was some kind of revenge play by Webber. But then I realized it didn't have anything to do with me at all. It was about *them*.

"Once she ran out of threads she knew, she chose each of you for a specific purpose. For example, she took Lily because she thought a child might save her son. The others must have suited her requirements in other ways. I don't pretend to fully understand her rationale." Kismet lets out a gasp, but I keep going. The time for sorrow has passed. This is the time for joy.

"Kismet, when I created you, you were the most brilliant thread the heavens had ever seen. Souls came from other departments just to look at you. Webber, the Weaver, couldn't make you blend into the tapestry of life no matter how hard he worked. A sparkler, that's what we called you.

"And Andrew, you complemented her in every way. You two went together. I think Mara chose the two of you because she couldn't take her eyes off you. Nothing more, nothing less."

Kismet snorted a little. "Lucky us."

"Sometimes, those who are special pay a higher price for their uniqueness," Horatia says.

Laughing at the sour face Kismet makes, I say, "I knew you could handle it."

She sticks her tongue out at me.

"Will we see you again?" she asks, but I can tell by the wistful expression on Andrew's face that he already knows the answer.

"No, my love."

Kismet falls into my arms, and Andrew wraps both of us into a big bear hug. "I don't want to lose you," she says through her tears.

"You won't. You'll find me in your happiness."

She pulls away. I see that they both have tears in their eyes, but strangely, mine are dry. Suddenly, I'm not mourning them anymore. I'm happy for them. Their trials are finally over. And so are mine.

As if they can sense we're ready, the gates of heaven open, and angels step out to usher Andrew and Kismet into their forever. Horatia and I stand back, arms around each other, watching them go. I feel nothing but complete happiness as I see my two greatest creations walk into paradise together.

TWENTY-FOUR

Michaela

Seeing Lily off was so satisfying. Galenia and I walk back to my quarters with our arms linked, almost skipping. But another Reaper interrupts us on the way.

"Michaela. It's good to see you," he says, a warm smile on his face.

I recognize him. He's been with us for a while.

"Lyall. It's good to see you," I say, holding out my hand.

Smiling at the Reaper, Galenia releases me and says, "I'll leave you here."

"Thank you for everything, Galenia," I say, and she embraces me with her whole heart.

"We'll see each other soon," she assures me.

I watch her go, and it's like looking at an angel. She really is a special creation.

"She's something," Lyall says, unable to resist watching her too.

"That she is." I turn my attention back to him. "What can I do for you, Lyall?"

"Ryker would like to see you right away."

"Oh. Of course."

Once his message is delivered, he shifts uncomfortably, not sure what else to say. "I really am glad you're back," he says earnestly.

I laugh. "I believe you. Thank you for the message, Lyall. I'll make my way there now."

He nods and leaves me.

To my surprise, Penn meets me outside of Ryker's office.

"Penn. What are you doing here? Did Kismet and Andrew get off okay?"

"Ryker has something to say to us apparently." I sense a bit of mischief in his eyes, but he keeps talking, distracting me from it. "And yes, they did. It was harder than I thought it would be. But somehow, it was easy too. It felt right."

I reach for his hand, and he takes it. "Just like this feels right," he says.

I look up at him, searching for his meaning, when it suddenly hits me that he's wearing his Spinner's uniform once more. I guess he's done hiding. It makes my heart race even faster to see him unmasked. But before I can demand to know why he's suddenly on a suicide mission, Ryker bellows for us to come in.

"Ah. Michaela. Penn. Good to see you again. Please, sit down."

Penn. He called him Penn. He knows.

I take measured steps toward the white chair, and Penn sits in the black one. I'm struggling to control my breathing, but Penn seems very relaxed. Why doesn't he care more about his fate? Does he feel like there's nothing left to live for now that Kismet and Andrew are gone?

"Why so nervous?" Ryker asks, looking directly at me. He's smiling, which doesn't set me at ease at all. He knows a secret, one he's obligated to tell, that will destroy one of my best friends.

My eyes immediately go to Penn, and Ryker starts laughing. *Laughing.* Something snaps inside me.

"How can you be so coldhearted, Ryker? After everything we've been through together?" He stops laughing immediately, and his expression turns serious. I sit up straighter, ready to defend my outburst.

"Michaela, my dear Reaper. Why would you think I'm cold?"

"Because you're laughing about what's going to happen to Penn." Suddenly, I'm unsure of myself. Could I be wrong?

"No, I'm laughing at *you*, Michaela."

"But thank you for coming to my defense so readily," Penn adds.

They're in on something together. Confused, I look back and forth between the two of them. "What's going on?"

"Penn is not going to be destroyed. In fact, I have a proposal for him."

Penn raises an eyebrow at Ryker. "Oh, really?"

"Yes. I've made an arrangement with creation. You could work in management there. Help determine what orders to send to the Fates, what types of people are needed on Earth. I think your experience on Earth would make you an excellent fit for the position."

Penn is silent, and so am I. Words have failed me. Could Penn really return to work here in the heavens without facing any consequences?

"But wouldn't they know who he was?" I ask.

"They already know who he is," Ryker says with a small smile. "He is safe, Michaela. He's received a full pardon."

"What?" I yell, jumping out of my seat. "Why didn't you tell me? Why wasn't that the *first* thing out of your mouth when I saw you outside the office?"

"You were firing off so many questions, I couldn't get a word in edgewise," he says, laughing as I hug him and jump around, jostling him roughly, I'm sure.

I pull away and look at him through tears of joy. "It's been a long time since we've had such joyful news. We need to sing this from all corners of the heavens!"

"We will. But there are things to discuss first," he says. He nods toward Ryker, who's smiling from ear to ear.

"You," I say, looking at Ryker "You really had me going." He laughs, and I glance from him to Penn with daggers in my eyes.

Finally, I let my face settle into a smile. "So now what?" I ask

Penn. "You move on to creation?"

"Maybe. Maybe not. I've been thinking of retirement." His words make me sit back in my seat. I have to admit, it's something I've been considering too. I'm not sure how I can go on after everything that's happened. Shiloh felt like a good place to stop, the perfect ending. But what am I going to do with myself if I stop Reaping?

"I was thinking of traveling around Earth," Penn says. "Not settling in like Fia did, but exploring. Seeing all the things you've seen on your Reapings."

I sigh wistfully. It sounds wonderful. Relaxing. Energizing.

Ryker is eyeing me, a look of consideration on his face.

"But I couldn't do it without a guide," Penn says, also watching me.

I sit up straighter and look at him. Is he being serious? "Did you just proposition me?"

"Only if you want to come."

"Now, just hold on a minute. Let me plead my case before you make any hasty decisions," Ryker says quickly.

I look to him, my heart racing again, but for a completely different reason this time. I'm not panicking at all, not as I constantly have been for so long. I'm...excited. Suddenly, it feels as if the possibilities that extend before me are endless.

"Michaela, you are one of the best Reapers the heavens have ever seen," Ryker says. "I don't want to lose you to some hippie Fate who wants to wander the Earth like a vagabond."

"Hey," Penn says, feigning hurt.

Ryker ignores him. "Should you choose to go to Earth, you will be taken care of forever. You will have everything you need financially and otherwise. Despite how enticing that may sound, I have a place for you in upper management among the Reapers. You'd be working *with* me, not for me, and managing the Reapers and the other departments."

"So...I wouldn't be Reaping anymore?" I say, not sure how I feel about staying in the heavens, but not Reaping.

"No. But you'd be helping others, teaching them how to do a better job, passing your centuries of knowledge on to the next generation of Reapers."

He knows me well. It's tempting to seize the opportunity to play a part in the greater story of the heavens. Penn sits silently, letting me make my decision for myself.

I'm not sure how much time passes while I sit in silence, pondering my options. But it boils down to this—I can't imagine my life in the heavens if I'm not Reaping. And while I'm sure Ryker would let me reap if I asked to continue, I'm ready for something new. Something different. They're short a Spinner, and I could probably try that for a bit, but I know I wouldn't be as good as Penn and fear I'd be as bad as Webber.

The only thing that puts a smile on my face is the thought of returning to Earth. And the prospect of spending the rest of my existence there with Penn makes my smile grow even wider.

"Please, take all the time you want to think about it," Ryker says, trying to play his cards right.

"No. I'm ready," I say, although I pause a bit before saying what, exactly, I'm ready for.

They sit in anxious silence, waiting for me to claim my own fate.

"I think Penn's idea sounds lovely. I'd like to travel a bit."

Ryker sits back in his seat, defeated. "Well, if you two ever change your minds, you will always be welcome here."

Penn turns to him in surprise. "Really? But Fia made it sound like once you were on Earth, you were there for good."

"Yes, well, that was supposed to apply to all banished souls too, and you proved to be an exception to that rule, didn't you?" Ryker answers with a sly grin.

My former boss turns to face me. "You know how to reach me." Standing, he holds his hand out across his desk, but I circle the wood and embrace him instead. His arms fall around me, and I feel their weight. He's a big man, and he envelops me completely, keeping me safe, just as he has for centuries.

"Thank you, Ryker. For everything."

He pulls away and looks at me with eyes so dark, I can't tell where his irises stop and his pupils start. "Thank *you*, Michaela. You have been a true blessing to all of us."

I smile, and Penn and I walk out together. There's only one thing left to do. The hardest part—say goodbye.

We arrive at the Fates' workroom after a silent walk across the heavens. I wonder what Penn is thinking about, but I don't want to interrupt his thoughts. He hesitates outside the door, which stands open. I can see Galenia sitting at her low desk, staring off into space, but I can't see Horatia from my vantage point. I'm sure she's sharpening her scissors or something. A companionable silence hangs between them.

Penn doesn't interrupt the Fates at first. He leans against the doorway, arms folded, watching them with a smirk on his face. We both know it will be a long time before we see them again, if ever, and I know he's relishing the sight of them in this space they shared for centuries.

Horatia spots him first. "Well, don't you look sharp?"

Galenia rushes over to us. "Are you coming back?" she asks excitedly.

"No. Haven't they assigned Webber a replacement yet?" Penn asks, concern written deeply in the wrinkles of his forehead.

Horatia is quick to answer. "No, but they will. I hear they have some very promising trainees. Mostly women. Might be nice for this to be a girls' club again." She hip checks Penn, and he laughs.

"So far, they're blaming the population lull on some uterine virus that's making people barren. A miracle doctor will come along soon and things will get moving again, don't you worry."

Penn nods, but I can tell he doesn't like it.

"So, what will you do?" Galenia asks.

"Travel. See the world. See everything I didn't get to see last time," he answers.

Something is bothering me though. Has anyone even asked the sister Fates what they want? "Are you guys okay with staying here? With continuing to work?" I ask carefully, eyeing them both.

Galenia is the first to answer. "Yes, I'm excited to get back to work. To contribute." I can't help but smile at her, knowing she is exactly where she's meant to be.

Horatia hesitates. "I'm not ready to go. Not yet." She looks fondly at Galenia. "Besides, I couldn't leave her alone."

Galenia puts her arm around Horatia's neck. "I do appreciate that. But far be it from me to hold you back."

Horatia sticks her tongue out at her smaller sister, and we all laugh together one last time.

EPILOGUE

Michaela

Fiji is lovely. The warm, white sands feel luxurious beneath my toes. The water in front of me is crystal clear, and huge mountains and lush greenery sprawl out behind me, teaming with life. Penn, who's standing across from me, sends me a brilliant smile.

We've been on Earth a few months now, but this is our first time in Fiji. I must admit, I could stay here a while.

Cody, Aida, and their family sit in white folding chairs next to an aisle lined with beautiful pink orchids. They are thrilled, and the youngest girl, Kareena, waves wildly at Fia. The bride smiles warmly and waves back with the hand that's holding her bouquet. There are only a handful of other people in the audience.

Fia resisted Wyatt at first, which Penn thought was hilarious. By the time we stopped in to visit them in New York, Wyatt had settled into her apartment, and although she claimed she wanted nothing to do with him, she also said she made him a boxed lunch ever day before she left for work at the temple. When she chastised herself for getting soft, Penn said he knew Wyatt had won her over.

When Wyatt asked me to stand next to him, I wasn't sure. Although I do owe him a debt for saving my life from a band of ghosts desperate to use my life force to find their way home, it seemed like someone else would be better suited for such an occasion—a brother, or perhaps an old college pal. But he insisted. He said, "Fia's gonna have some fancy Fate on her side. I think I should have someone from the heavens on my side too. It's only fair. After all, you're sort of my kind. I mean, we work in the same department." After I finished laughing, I found myself saying yes.

Fia admitted she was nervous about taking a human husband. I think her exact words were, "I don't want to watch him die. I have better things to do than take care of some old man."

Wyatt just laughed and said, "Honey, don't you worry about taking care of me. Just learn to keep up."

That was when I knew if anyone was right for her, it was Wyatt.

As I watch them exchange their vows, I feel...calm. In my short time on Earth, a peace has fallen over me unlike anything I've ever experienced. Before all this happened, I was blissfully unaware of the turmoil life can bring, so I can't say I was at peace. Not really. But I looked into the depths of darkness and still saw the light. I know the worst that can happen, and I came out on the other side, and let me tell you, it looks pretty good from here.

NAMES

Aida: Helper. Cody's wife and sister to Cedric.

Andrew: Warrior or strength. Kismet's true love.

Cody: Helpful. Aida's husband, who helps Penn out of the swamp.

Chesney: Peaceful. One of the surprise names.

Eve: Lively or life. Cody and Aida's oldest (and first) daughter.

Fia: Weaver. The woman Penn replaced as Spinner.

Frederico: Peaceful. One of the names on the list of surprises

Galenia: Small and intelligent. The third Fate who decides how a life will end.

Heth: Trembling fear. Michaela's enemy, instigator among the Reapers.

Horatia: Timekeeper. The second Fate who decides how long a life will be.

Jeff: Divinely peaceful. Second name on the list of surprises.

Kismet: Destiny. Andrew's true love.

Lily: Pure. Child Michaela is assigned to take, and the last surprise.

Lyall: Loyal. Reaper who meets Michaela toward the end.

Mara: Bitter. The human.

Michaela: Feminine of Michael, the angel of death. The Reaper.

Miette: Small, sweet thing. Michaela's Reaper friend.

Nathair: Snake. Reaper who's on leave/missing.

Nysa: New beginning. The first surprise name, the first to have her thread cut short.

Pearl: Precious stone. One of the names on the list of surprises.

Penn: Masculine form of Penelope, meaning Weaver. First of the three Fates, the Spinner.

Ryker: Strength. Reaper's boss.

Shiloh: Shiloh was where a critical battle took place during the American Civil War. Additionally, the Hebrew translation of this word is 'the one to whom it belongs.' Shiloh is the human's—Mara's—child.

Wyatt: Guide. Ghost hunter who saves Michaela.

Webber: Weaver. Penn's rival who's promoted to Spinner when Penn is banished.

Meanings found using basic Google searches and Meaningof-Names.com

Did you enjoy this book?
Be sure and leave a review!

ACKNOWLEDGEMENTS

Number nine. I can't believe *The Human* is my ninth published book. What a long way we've all come together. I've lost some folks, and gained some great ones along the way, so obviously, I have a lot to be thankful for.

First, and foremost, I extend my eternal gratitude to God. I know my thanks here are inadequate when compared to my many blessings, but I am so unbelievably grateful. And I pray I never forget that gratitude, because I am entitled to nothing.

Let me tell you something. My husband Dan is a total rock star. See, we are not very compatible people. I thrive on affection, and he needs his space. We are rock meets hard place. Yet, he is my constant supporter and cheerleader. He handles all my marketing, and he is the main reason *The Reaper* had such a great release. It was his ideas that gave it the extra push to hit number two on Amazon's Hot New Releases list. He's amazing, right? Get your own, dear reader. I'm not giving him up.

As always, my parents are staunch supporters. I hope I can always live up to the pride they have in me. It's an amazing feeling, guys, and I hope you have someone in your life who reminds you how awesome you are just like they do for me.

My friends, Mary, Dannie, and Christian. How could I have ever gotten this far without you? Nine books you've had to hear me complain about, tell plotlines to and act like you understood, and listen as I told you about bad reviews and my many other setbacks. You laughed and cried with me, and for that, I'm eternally grateful.

You should know that this isn't all me. This magic doesn't happen on my own. I have an *amazing* team of people behind me with the best brand of turd polish I've ever seen. Specifically, Angela and Cynthia, your ability to see through my gobbletygook and make it something not only readable, but also amazing, is astounding.

Lastly, you, dear reader. Thank you for giving me your most valuable asset—your time. You've spent the last two hundred or so pages with me, and I hope you've enjoyed the ride as much as I did. (Insert evil laugh about what happened to Mara here.)

I'll see you in September. (Did you sing that part? Because you should've.)

—*S*

ABOUT THE AUTHOR

Stephanie Erickson is an English Literature graduate from Flagler College. She lives in Florida with her family. *The Human* is her ninth novel.

She loves to connect with readers! Follow her on Facebook at http://www.facebook.com/stephmerickson, Twitter @ sm_erickson, or stop by her Web site at www.stephanieericksonbooks.com.

You can also get the latest news on new releases, contests, and author appearances by signing up for her newsletter on her Web site.

STEPHANIE'S BOOKS